THE HAU
OF
REDBURN
MANOR

ALSO BY

EVE S EVANS

Fiction:

The Haunting of Hartley House

Hartley House Homecoming

The Haunting of Crow House

Anthologies:

True Ghost Stories of First Responders

50 Terrifying Ghost Stories

Real Ghost Stories

Shadow People

Chilling Ghost Stories

Haunted Hotels

Haunted Hospitals

Haunted Objects

Haunted People

Haunted Suburbs

Voices From Beyond

This book is dedicated to my partner in crime. Thank you for all of your help when I need to bounce ideas around. You are the best!

Follow Eve and her books on Goodreads or Bookbub! And get notified of any new reads coming in 2021.

The following story is fictional. Any resemblance to real persons, places, things, or events is merely coincidental.

Cover By: Penny Dreadful

Hey, you recording yet?"

Randall grunted, still fiddling with the laptop as he set up the live stream. "Give me a minute," he muttered. "Wifi's being slow."

Nathan clicked his tongue impatiently, glancing at the others. "You know what to do?"

Avery rolled her eyes. "How long have we been doing this?"

"Alright, alright. Just making sure," Nathan said, holding out his hands defensively. "Lucy can kick us off, yeah?"

"Sure!"

"Alright, and we're live in 3… 2… 1."

"Hey there, ghost streamers," Lucy started, her voice echoing faintly around the open dining room. "What an exciting end to our investigation. We've caught a ton of evidence here that we're super excited to share with you."

Nathan nodded, chiming in: "Bixbee Mansion has been a place long renowned in the history books for its tragic past, and during our stay we got a glimpse of what it must have been like living here."

"Don't forget, all of the evidence we captured will be uploaded onto our website for you to look at, so let us know your thoughts in the comments. Did we capture evidence of paranormal activity at Bixbee Mansion?" Randall said cryptically, grinning at the camera. "I think you'll be pretty impressed with what we got."

Lucy shuffled the notes in her hand, taking her cue from Nathan. "Alright then, let's start with a little history lesson on Bixbee Mansion, before we get into the meat of the investigation," she said. "The house was built in the early 1800s by one Henry Bixbee, a man we actually know very little about. The house's early history is somewhat difficult to find, but it stayed in the Bixbee family until the early 1900s. During the first World War, it was actually used as a hospital to support the excessive number of injured soldiers, and so these rooms witnessed a lot of illness and death. Many soldiers died here due to their wounds, and some of that negative energy still lingers today. A man named Rupert Thompson is one of those whose spirit is said to haunt the mansion, and some of the evidence we caught suggests that we managed to make contact with him. Randall, do you want to play that?"

Randall nodded, fiddling with the audio on the laptop and playing the EVP they had recorded on their second night of investigation.

"Can you tell us your name?" Avery's voice came through on the audio, slightly muffled against the background static.

A few moments later, there was a faint whisper, clear enough to distinguish a man's voice. "Rupert."

"Did you die here?"

Again, there was crackly silence for a while, and then another whisper, slightly broken up. "Bu…llet."

Randall stopped the audio and Lucy glanced back down at her notes. "Rupert Thompson died from a severe shrapnel wound after many days of suffering alone in one of the temporary hospital rooms. We also managed to record an EVP of a child speaking to us. We unearthed in our records that the original

Henry Bixbee had a niece called Lily, who died here from poor health in 1821. It may be possible that it was her voice we captured during our investigation."

She flicked a glance at Randall, who pulled up the second audio file with a few clicks of the laptop.

"Did you used to live here?" This time it was Nathan's voice asking the question.

There was a soft whine of static.

"Were you here when the house was a hospital?"

Then a child's spoke in a low, harsh whisper. "Bad… place…"

Randall stopped the audio. "We hear the child saying 'bad place' in this clip, though we're not entirely sure what she might be referring to. We later uncovered the secret that Lily's illness might not have been entirely accidental, either. Henry's brother, and Lily's father, was known to be a cruel man who didn't much care for his wife and daughter. While this is mostly speculation, given the child's warning of the house being a 'bad place', it is possible that something more sinister happened here during the residence of the Bixbee family."

Nathan picked up then, talking about some of the experiences he'd had during the stay. "During the second night, I actually had something tug on the back on my shirt. We replayed the clip several times, and there's nothing in the environment that could have caused it."

"During our three day stay here," Avery finished up, "we've collected a range of evidence. And we think it's safe to say that Bixbee Mansion lives up to its haunted reputation. Is it possible the ghost of Lily Bixbee and Rupert Thompson, as well as countless other soldiers, reside here after their deaths? We think so."

"And that's it from us today. This is Avery, Lucy, Nate and Randall, coming at you live from Bixbee Mansion. Stay tuned for next week's episode, where we'll be investigating a house that has seen over two hundred years of murder, suicide and death."

The car skidded to a stop with a sudden lurch, and something thudded against the floor of the trunk. Avery jerked forward in her seat, catching herself against the headrest in front of her, and shot John, their driver, a narrow look.

The man smiled sheepishly, brushing a piece of curling grey hair away from his face. "Sorry," he said. "Hope none of your equipment got damaged."

"I'm sure it's fine," Nathan said with a dismissive wave, unclipping his seat belt. "Thanks for the ride. You remember when you're picking us up?"

"End of the week," John said. "Friday."

Nathan nodded and reached over to open his door. In the back, Randall, Lucy and Avery groaned and stretched as they shuffled out of the car. They'd spent the two hour car journey squashed together with their luggage that couldn't fit in the trunk.

Avery stretched her arms over her head, hearing her shoulder joints pop. "Glad that's over," she muttered, going round the back of the car to help Randall unload the bags.

Nathan propped his hands on his hips with a mystified look on his face. "I thought the journey was fine. Pretty comfy if you ask me."

The three of them shot him a look, and he cowered with a grin. "Alright, alright, you can fight over the front seat next time."

Hauling their bags onto the pavement beside the car, Randall shut the trunk and they waved John off as he pulled away, saluting them in the wing mirror.

"Well, this is it," Lucy said. "We're here."

Nathan nodded at the house in front of them. "Redburn Manor, in all her beauty."

"More like fallen splendour," Lucy muttered, scanning her eyes over the grimy brown bricks, spiderwebbed with cracks and dirt. Ivy tumbled down one side of the house, pushing through the bricks with its long, spindly tendrils.

"There's a certain charm to it," Randall said with a shrug. "What do you think, Avery?"

The three of them turned to her, and she dragged her eyes away from the upper window, where she'd been staring. "Charming, yeah," she said distractedly.

"Well, shall we get inside then?" Nathan said, producing an old-fashioned key from his pocket.

"Lead the way."

It was already late in the afternoon by the time they'd arrived at the house, and although the air was warmed from the sun, grey clouds were banking in from the west, burgeoning with rain, and a chill had begun to blow, stirring leaves across the pavement.

Redburn Manor was a shadow blotted against the sky. An old, crumbling husk of something that was once grand and beautiful. It was a three-story building, with ornate turreted windows that now seemed drab and gloomy in the shade, the glass dirty and cracked in places.

As Nathan slid the key into the lock, Avery almost held her breath.

The door opened without a noise. Particles of disturbed dust flew up, glinting in the wavering light of the afternoon. Nathan shot the others a glance over his shoulder before being the first to step inside. Randall followed, then Lucy.

Avery waited another few seconds before she too stepped forward. From where she was stood, the entryway stretched down into semi-darkness. The sunlight that had been warming her back before dipped behind one of those dark clouds, and the wind stirred strands of hair across her face.

"You coming?" Lucy asked, glancing over her shoulder when she noticed Avery hadn't followed.

Schooling her features into a more casual pose, she nodded and stepped in after them.

The sensation of dust on her skin was the first thing she noticed; it itched along her arms and tickled the back of her throat, making her cough. The place had been shut up for a long time, after its last stint as a Bed and Breakfast a few years ago. After the last tragedy happened, the place sunk into its own despair, becoming a place nobody cared for anymore.

"Woah!" Randall said from further inside. "This place is huge!" His voice echoed along the high-vaulted ceiling, stirring the cobwebs that latticed the rafters. There was a staircase on the left, which stretched up into darkness, and on her right, an old-fashioned mirror with gilded edges that was obscured by dust and old fingerprints.

Lucy ran a finger along its edge, pulling away a streak of muck.

"Back when it was a Bed and Breakfast, this place was able to accommodate up to twenty people," she said as she used the sleeve of her jacket to wipe away some of the dirty prints on the glass. Avery watched the reflection clear, showing her the staircase on the opposite side. Mirrors were often said to hold a lot of spiritual energy, and she made a note to keep an eye on it.

"I thought it was a hotel?" Randall said.

"That was before it became a Bed and Breakfast. Neither businesses lasted very long."

"And before any of that, it served as a mental institution," Nathan added, his teeth flashing in the dark.

The rest of them shared a glance, half-uncertain smiles creeping along their faces. Places like mental institutions and hospitals – where people were usually sick and not very well cared for – were often imbued with negative energies far more than other buildings. Emotions like fear and grief and anger could be soaked up by old houses, continuing to manifest in such ways for years to come.

On the street outside, they all heard the rumble of a car engine, and the faint squeal of tires as it pulled up against the curb.

"That'll be Caroline," Lucy said, breaking the silence. "I'll go see if she needs any help with her bags."

Lucy disappeared back outside, while Avery lingered behind the other two, taking in every detail of the entryway. She could feel the weight of the house's grandeur, even amongst the dust and shadows. She figured this must have been a beautiful house once, home to an aristocratic family. But then it had been sold off and adopted into a temporary mental institution in the late 1800s and early 1900s. That's when its real history begins as a place synonymous with tragic death and suicide. The reason they were there, investigating the rumours and stories that had been shared over the years.

"Where do you want to set up base?" Nathan asked as he poked his head into the door on his right, pulling away with a sniff. "Ugh, this place hasn't been cleaned in years."

"Wherever has the least dust," Randall said with a shrug.

The door behind them opened again, shedding watery grey light into the landing. Avery noticed for the first time the hummingbirds printed on the wallpaper. In the strange light, they looked too thin and lanky.

"Hi guys," Caroline said as she came through, brushing aside a strand of pale yellow hair.

"Hey Carol," Nathan said, lifting his hand. "Good journey?"

"Yeah, traffic wasn't too bad," she said absently, lugging a bag after her and setting it down by her feet with a huff.

"Next time, I'm travelling with you," Randall muttered, shaking his head. "John's driving is getting worse."

Caroline chuckled, and Lucy came in after her with another black bag strung around her shoulder.

"What have you got in here?" She said, struggling to lower it to the floor.

"Psychic things," she said with a wink, chuckling. "I like to come prepared, that's all."

"Let's get set up and do an introductory session," Nathan suggested, leading the group further into the house. Passing the room

Nathan had glanced in before, Avery paused to peer inside. Although the curtains were open, there wasn't much light in the room, and it was heavy with the scent of mildew. Old, rotted furniture and moth-eaten sheets and not much else.

She pulled away, throwing a smile at Caroline over her shoulder, and followed the two men into the large sitting room at the end of the hall.

"Looks cosy. Want to set up our equipment in here?"

"Sure."

Randall lugged a black duffel bag onto the coffee table beside an ornate fireplace, being careful not to be too heavy handed. Their equipment was expensive, and they probably couldn't afford replacements if anything got damaged.

Avery looked around in awe, admiring the decorated ceiling panels and the silver-edged chandelier suspended from the middle of the room. "Must've been one posh Bed and Breakfast," she muttered to nobody in particular. "I'm surprised all this stuff is still here."

"Well, after what happened to the previous owners, I guess nobody ever came back to clear it all up," Lucy said.

While Nathan and the others began to set up the recording equipment, Avery went over and grabbed a fistful of the heavy red curtains obscuring the window. As she drew them aside, a cloud of dust billowed out from them. She let go, spluttering as she tried to wave the dust away from her eyes and nose.

"You alright over there?" Nathan asked.

She shot a thumbs up over her shoulder. "G-great," she wheezed, dragging the rest of the curtains aside to let in a thin stream of afternoon light. The clouds had descended thick and fast, covering most of the sky, and the room was still just as gloomy as before.

A draught was coming in from somewhere too, and Avery backed away from the window rubbing her arms. "I take it there's no central heating," she said. "Do you think there's any fuel for that fire?" She nodded towards the hearth, where the grate bled nothing but dry ash.

"Huh, good point. Does the place have an outhouse? Storeroom?" Randall said. "There might be some wood left around. As long as it hasn't been exposed to damp, it should still light."

"I'll go take a look," Avery suggested. She wanted to see more of the house anyway.

"I'll come with you," Caroline added. There was an uncertain edge to her expression, and Avery was curious to hear what the psychic was feeling about the house so far.

The two women left the sitting room in silence. Avery checked the cupboard beneath the stairs first, which harboured nothing but some old, mildewed furniture, and then the utility room, but there was no firewood. There was a door in the kitchen that led into the field at the rear of the property, so their last bet was if the house had some kind of storage shed.

The door was on a latch that could only be opened from the inside, but it was rusty from disuse and took several attempts to wriggle it free.

"Is everything okay, Caroline?" Avery asked as she finally unlatched the door, pausing with her hand resting against it.

"Yeah, everything's fine. Just tired from the journey."

"You seemed a little worried back there. Was there something about the room?"

She said nothing for a moment, then nodded, her eyes turning a cloudy shade of blue-grey. “There was… something *off* about it. I can’t say what though. I just felt a little suffocated in there.”

Avery chewed her lip. Caroline’s predictions were never usually too far off the mark. If she felt uncomfortable in there, it was for a good reason.

“But I’m sure it’s nothing,” she added quickly. “I don’t like saying anything unless I’m certain of what I’m feeling. I didn’t spend long enough in there to really get a feel for the place.”

Avery said nothing as she pushed open the door, a gust of wind immediately blowing through. The air had turned cold since that morning. There was a sharp chill now, and the wind had picked up, dragging her hair out behind her.

Beside the main property was a small outhouse made of reddish-brown brick. There was a single window, but most of it was obscured by thick cobwebs, and something inside was partially blocking it.

“Looks like some kind of work shed,” Caroline said as the two of them approached it.

"I'm not sure if we'll find any wood inside, but it's worth a look."

"Let's hope it isn't locked," Avery added.

Caroline hummed in agreement, wrapping her arms around her waist as the wind picked up, scattering dry leaves across their path.

When they reached the shed, Avery hesitated before touching it. The door frame was swathed with cobwebs, and she could see little black husks of insects tucked away in the corners. But Caroline was shivering behind her, so she braved it and twisted the handle.

The door opened with a shudder, and a spider the size of her fingernail scuttled out from its web, causing Avery to flinch back. Caroline chuckled behind her. "Want me to go first?"

Avery grimaced at her childish display in front of the older woman, but nodded anyway, stepping aside to let Caroline pass.

The psychic went first, squinting as her eyes adjusted to the darkness inside, and Avery followed, careful not to brush her arms against the doorframe.

Inside the air smelt musty and damp, and when she glanced up, Avery could see a stain forming in the roof where water had been coming in. "If there is any wood in here, I'm not sure it'll be dry," she said, blowing out a sigh.

"Maybe not," Caroline said hopefully. "Look, under the workbench."

Avery followed her gaze to a small log store under the bench, tucked away in the shadows between a toolbox and an old-fashioned lawn mower.

"There might not be much inside, but I reckon it'll be better than freezing to death."

With the help of Avery, Caroline managed to drag the box out, pushing the lid onto the ground. A meagre stash of firewood was tucked inside, flaky but still dry. "This'll do," she said, picking up an armful of wood.

As Avery moved to grab the rest, something caught her attention and she whipped around.

For just a moment, it looked like someone had been peering through the window. It was only a glance in her periphery, but she was sure she had seen someone stood there.

Without a word, she left Caroline and darted back outside, turning wildly to see if anyone else was out there with them. But the field stretched on for miles, the long grass blowing in the wind, and there was nobody else around.

"Avery! You okay?" Caroline asked as she ran out after her a moment later.

"I… I thought I saw something," she said, turning to look at the window from the outside. Maybe she'd imagined it, or it had just been the wind, but she couldn't get the image out of her head that something had been there. "Never mind. It must have been nothing."

"You sure?" Caroline asked, glancing around them as the breeze stirred the grasses around their feet, bending the treetops in the distance.

"I'm sure. Come on, let's get back to the others."

The fire crackled low in the fireplace as the five of them sat huddled around it, warming their hands against the heat.

Randall was fiddling with the recording equipment, setting up the camera for their livestream. They usually kicked off with an introductory podcast for the case they were working, giving details of the house and what they were hoping to find.

"Okay, that should do it!" He said, twisting the laptop around so they could see the stream. "You ready to start?"

"Go ahead," Nathan said. "I'll introduce, then we'll cut to Lucy for a history lesson, and Avery and Caroline can say a bit more about the house itself. Sound good?"

They all nodded, and Randall hit the button to record.

"Hey ghost streamers, we're live here at Redburn Manor, a place haunted for years by the unfortunate patients of the Redburn Mental

Institution that closed its doors back in the mid-1900s. Lucy's here to tell you more about the house's sinister history."

Lucy cleared her throat, leaning closer to the microphone. In the firelight, her cheeks glowed red and her eyes were deeply shadowed, casting an eerie visage on the screen. "Redburn Manor was built in the late 1800s by a man called Philip Redburn. He lived here with his family until 1926, when it was sold off and bought by a wealthy psychiatrist who wanted to open up his own medical practice. The house retained the name of its original owner, becoming the Redburn Mental Institute, more colloquially known as the Redburn Asylum. At the height of the late 1940s, lobotomies and other practices were becoming more widespread in these institutions, and we have records that the staff here practised a lot of maltreatment on their patients. While we'll never be completely sure what went on behind these walls, a lot of patients died from neglect and health complications following the experimental practises conducted on them. The Asylum eventually shut its doors in the mid-1950s, and almost twelve years later was bought by a business entrepreneur with plans to refurbish the place into a modern hotel. The hotel saw brief success upon its opening, but quickly succumbed to rumours and stories about the place being haunted. Residents of the hotel reported hearing whispers in the middle of the night, and the sound of scratching on the walls. Some heard the wheels of a trolley being pushed along linoleum in the middle of the night, and one resident even reported seeing an apparition of a patient."

Avery felt a chill touch the back of her neck. Asylums were known for the negative energies that lingered inside them, and even after this place had been refurbished several times, she had no doubt some of that energy remained. That's why it had been dogged by rumours and sightings all these years.

"After the hotel went bankrupt, it was snatched up in the late 1990s by a couple who had plans to turn it into a classy Bed and Breakfast, catering for customers higher on the pay scale. Like the hotel, the business boomed into the early 2000s, until its sordid history caught up with it and it succumbed to the same fate as the Redburn Hotel. It finally shut its doors in 2013 and has lain dormant since."

As Lucy wrapped up the house's history, Nathan looked expectantly at Avery and Caroline. The two women exchanged a glance, and Avery saw from the look on the psychic's face that she wasn't quite ready to speak.

Avery cleared her throat, looking towards the camera. "You can tell nobody's come back since the B&B closed down," she started with an encouraging nod from Nathan. "There's a definite feeling of neglect about the place, as though it's been forgotten about for a long time. It's a very dark house too. Even with all of the windows, it doesn't seem to let in much light. Almost as though the shadows are too thick to let any through." Realising she was rambling, she cleared her throat again, shuffling in her seat. "Knowing about the place's history as an asylum has definitely skewed my perception of the house. I don't see it as a hotel or a bed and breakfast, but as a hospital where unwell patients didn't get the help they needed." She cast a lingering glance on the window, where the sun was beginning to set beyond the grey clouds. Even the last rays of watery golden light barely penetrated farther than the windowsill. "I think the manor's history as an asylum is like a stain you can't wash out. It lingers here, even after all these years have passed since it closed down. I expect we're going to uncover a lot more of the house's darker past during our investigations."

"You got that right," Nathan said, winking at the camera. Then he turned to the rest of the room and rose his voice: "I hope you give us a show tonight, ghosties. We've come all this way to see you."

Avery frowned at Nathan's taunt, but Randall and Lucy chuckled.

Somewhere deeper in the house, a door suddenly slammed shut, the reverberations trembling through the walls.

The five of them fell silent, and Avery felt her heartbeat quicken, her eyes going wide. She hadn't expected a direct response.

Lucy looked just as taken aback as her, but both Nathan and Randall burst into laughter.

"That's what I'm talking about," Nathan said.

"Nathan," Avery warned quietly, and he sobered, the laughter dying out.

"Well, it looks like we're not alone here after all," he continued, lowering his voice. "We have a long night ahead of us, so we'll catch up with you later. This is Nathan, Randall, Avery, Lucy and Caroline, signing out."

Randall finished up the recording, and the fire gave a loud pop as a piece of firewood tumbled down the pile, making Avery flinch.

"What do you think that was?" Lucy asked, glancing towards the doorway. "I don't remember any windows being open from the outside."

Nathan shrugged. "It could've been a breeze. Or, you know, it could have been something else. That's what we're here to find out, right?"

Lucy nodded, and Avery glanced across at Caroline. She'd been quiet for the last few minutes.

"Caroline?" She said, seeing the psychic frozen in a position with her back ramrod straight, her eyes resting on one corner of the room. "Everything okay?"

"I… I can feel something," she said, her voice oddly strained. "There's something here in the room with us… I don't know what. It's like it's…. watching us. Watching and waiting."

Her words sent a chill over the room, and the four podcasters shuffled uneasily. Caroline was a more recent addition to their podcast group, and although she didn't always join in with their camaraderie, they all respected her and her ability to sense things. None of them had reason to doubt anything she said.

"Do you know what it is?"

She shook her head, finally dragging her eyes away from the corner to look at them. She clenched her hands in her lap. "No. I can't decipher it. I can just… feel it. I felt it as soon as we came in here. There's something here, but I can't tell what it wants."

The stayed quiet. The fire dimmed with another crackle.

"I'm getting tired," Lucy said suddenly, covering up a yawn. "I think I'm going to unpack and catch up on some rest."

Avery stood with her. "Me too," she said. "Let's head up together." They were sharing a room with double beds on the first floor. Caroline had a room to herself, and the two men had one further down the hall.

They bid goodnight to the others and headed upstairs in silence.

The room they were staying in had been one of the old guest rooms, and while it retained some of its former cosiness, the added layer of dust and gloom to everything made the place uninviting. Other than the two beds, there was a dresser and a nightstand, and an old-fashioned brass lamp that was missing its bulb. Through the window, the last vestiges of daylight disappeared, and the room sunk into darkness. Avery reached into her bag and pulled out a battery-powered nightlight, setting it on the side so that they could see what they were doing.

"What do you think so far?" Lucy asked as Avery pulled a blanket out of her bag and spread it over the duvet.

"I'm not sure," she said, slipping out of her jacket and immediately regretting it as the room's chill touched her bare arms. "I'm still trying to figure it out. Something about this place kind of puts me on edge. I guess it's not surprising, given its history."

Lucy stared ruminatively at the wall over Avery's shoulder. "And the door slamming? Just a coincidence, or something more?"

Avery pursed her lips. "I think it was too aptly timed to just be a coincidence. But I can't say any more than that. Caroline seems to think there's something here, and I have no reason to doubt her judgement."

Lucy nodded, kicking off her shoes and sitting down on the end of the bed. The springs creaked beneath her. "I think you're right. I could kind of feel something too, when we came in. It's probably just some kind of intuition, but there might be something here after all." She nodded to herself, then shot Avery a crooked grin. "Well, I hope we manage to get some sleep tonight."

"Me too. If you need anything, wake me up, okay?"

"Goodnight Avery," she said as she climbed onto the bed, pulling the cover up to her chin.

Avery reached over and switched off the nightlamp, letting the shadows crawl along the room. "Night, Lucy."

It must have been the middle of the night when Avery woke up. Her eyes were thick with sleep, and the darkness seemed to swell around her like something alive, until she reached up and rubbed it away.

Something had woken her up.

She peeled her head from the pillow, aware of the sweat clinging to her skin, and tried to orientate herself.

In the silence of the room, she could hear something moving. A scuffling *crrk, crrrrk*, like something being dragged along the floor. Or… someone shuffling their feet. She listened harder, trying to work out what she was hearing. *Crrk, thmp, crrrk*.

Someone was in the room with them. Her body froze, and all she could move was her eyes, tracking around the room, trying to see what was making the noise. Every time her vision fuzzed with darkness, she blinked rapidly, trying to keep her breathing even as her heart thundered in her ears.

When her gaze fell on Lucy, her breathing hitched.

Someone was standing over her bed. In the darkness, she glimpsed a figure that was tall and thin, with a crooked nose and long hair cut out of shadow. It was leaning over Lucy's bed, watching her as she slept.

For a moment, all Avery could do was stare in horror, her throat clenching up and her heart thudding brutishly against her chest. Then a cry wrenched from her lips, shouting for Lucy to wake up.

The other woman jolted up with a gasp, and the figure dispersed into the shadows around the room.

Avery fumbled to switch on the nightlight, its warm blueish glow spreading around the room.

"W-what's going on?" Lucy said, squinting against the sudden light. "Avery?"

Avery said nothing, staring hard around the room to see where the figure had gone. They were alone.

The door shuddered open, and Nathan and Randall barged inside, their faces ghastly in the faint illumination. “Everything okay in here?”

“I don’t know. Avery woke me up,” Lucy said, rubbing her eyes and twisting to stare expectantly at the other woman.

Avery snapped out of her daze, blinking up at the others. “T-there was someone in here,” she stuttered, pulling her legs up to her chin. “I saw someone… standing over Lucy’s bed.”

Nathan and Randall glanced over at Lucy, but she seemed just as mystified.

“Are you sure you weren’t dreaming?” Nathan asked.

“No! I swear, I saw something.”

The two men exchanged a glance.

“I didn’t see anything,” Lucy said quietly, and Avery could sense they didn’t believe her. Now she was starting to doubt whether she had seen something herself. It had been dark, after all, and the visage had been hazy. Was it just her imagination conjuring things from the shadows?

“Anyway, try get some sleep, both of you,” Nathan said. “If you see anything else, wake us up okay?”

Avery nodded, and the two of them retreated from the room, shutting the door behind them.

Lucy turned to look at her from across the room, her eyes wide and pale in the nightlight. “Did you really see something?”

Avery sighed, lying back down. “I don’t know. Maybe.”

Lucy said nothing. After a few minutes, she turned over and went back to sleep.

Avery stared up at the ceiling. Her mind was wide awake now, and she had a feeling she wouldn’t be getting much more sleep that night. In her head, she kept seeing the figure standing over Lucy’s bed, watching her in silence. Had she really seen it?

She reached over to switch the nightlight off, then hesitated. It wouldn’t hurt to leave it on for now.

Chapter FOUR

Avery felt unrested and irritable the following morning. She hadn't been able to fall back asleep after waking up to that figure standing over Lucy's bed, and she'd spent most of the night trying to fathom whether or not what she had seen was real.

Although they'd had rain in the night, the sun was glinting off the windows that morning, but the light only stretched so far, and Avery could feel a chill from where she was standing in the kitchen.

"Wow, you look terrible," Nathan said when he saw her bloodshot eyes, the dark shadows on her skin.

She shot him a sarcastic smile. "Thanks."

"Seriously, though, you okay?"

Avery poured herself a cup of coffee from the pot that had just been brewed, stirring in far too much sugar. "Yeah. Just… had a bit of trouble falling back asleep last night."

Nathan said nothing, and she took her coffee to go and see Caroline in the main room.

"Morning," she said, coming to sit beside the psychic. "How'd you sleep last night?"

Caroline lifted her gaze from the papers she was reading and smiled, her eyes twinkling. "Not too bad. Thank you. How about yourself?"

"I don't know if the others told you," Avery said, sipping her coffee and grimacing as it burnt her tongue. "I woke up last night. Thought I saw something in our room."

Caroline's eyebrows arched. "What did you see?"

"I'm… not really sure. I thought I saw someone standing over Lucy's bed. It was just… watching her while she slept. It didn't do anything else."

A shadow passed across Caroline's face. "Did you see what it looked like?"

Avery hesitated, cradling her coffee cup as she tried to remember. It had been dark, but she recalled a few noticeable features. It had seemed tall and thin, and she remembered the long hair flowing out too.

"Why don't you take a look through the photos we have of the house?" Caroline suggested. "You might find a clue to their identity."

Avery's eyes brightened. "I think I might. Thanks, Caroline."

She returned to the documents she was reading – some old newspaper clippings judging by the yellowed pages – and Avery went to find Randall, who'd been the one to pack up all their photos and research notes.

"The property files?" Randall repeated when Avery flagged him down. "Sure, I'll get them for you." He rummaged around through one of the duffel bags and pulled out a manila folder. "Here you go. While you guys are down here, Nathan and I are going upstairs to investigate with some of the equipment."

Avery barely heard him. She took the files from his hand and staggered away, flipping through them as she went.

Randall watched her go with a frown.

"What's gotten into her?" Nathan asked from behind.

"Not sure. Maybe it has something to do with last night," he said, shrugging. "Anyway, you ready to head upstairs?"

Nathan hoisted the camera strap onto his shoulder and waved the EVP device around. "All set."

The two men climbed the stairs, and Randall pulled out a map he'd scrawled after looking at the house's old building plans.

"Okay, if I'm reading this correctly, the room on the left as we come up the stairs used to be one of the old operating rooms."

The handle got stuck when Nathan tried to turn it, and it took a couple of tries to get it open. The smell of damp wafted out, and Randall wrinkled his nose.

Booting up the thermal imaging camera, Nathan started recording as soon as he was in the room. "We're here in what was once an operating room of Redburn Metal Institute. Now it's a luxury master suite with a garden tub and walk-out balcony," he added, panning over the room for any heat signatures. "This is where the doctors would have performed surgeries on patients, including lobotomies," he added.

Randall hit record on the EVP device, going over to the bed in the corner of the room and sitting down on the edge. "Is there anyone in here who would like to speak with us?" He asked, shivering slightly. Although the curtains were drawn and the sun was streaming through the balcony, that corner of the room was particularly cold.

“My name’s Randall, and this is Nathan. Can you tell us your name?”

Nathan continued scanning the room with the camera, panning over to Randall to make sure it was picking up heat signatures as it should.

When he turned back around to face the balcony, he gave a start.

“Woah, hey, I’m picking something up here.”

Randall paused his EVP session and went over to look over Nathan’s shoulder. “What is it?”

A majority of the image on the screen was shades of blue and green, but in the centre was a red heat signature in the shape of a person. “No way,” he muttered.

Nathan grinned. “We actually got a person.”

It was a man, judging by the stature, and he was standing at the balcony doors, wavering slightly on the spot.

Then he began to move. Nathan and Randall watched with bated breath as the figure on the screen moved forward, passing straight through the balcony doors. He began to climb up the railings of the balcony, scrambling awkwardly with his hands and feet.

"Wait, what is he-"

Before Randall could finish, the figure threw himself off the balcony.

The abrupt loss of the heat signature made them both start, and then rushed to the balcony doors, throwing them wide.

The morning was mild, and although the sun was glinting down on them, both men shuddered as they glanced over the edge of the balcony railings.

The gravel drive below was empty. There was nobody there.

The two men stood in silence for a moment, staring down at the spot where the man must have landed.

"What did we just see?" Randall whispered, gooseflesh running along his skin.

"I don't know," Nathan said. "Some kind of residual haunting. A spirit reliving his death."

"He committed suicide," Randall said sadly. "But I can't believe we caught that on camera."

Nathan nodded, his eyes bright in the sun. "Only our first day of investigating and we've got some great footage. Our viewers are going to be pleased."

Avery stifled a yawn as she flicked through the pictures they'd managed to collate of the house during their preliminary preparations. Some of them were of the more recent renovations, but most of them were old black and white photographs taken back when the place had been Redburn Mental Institute. Thanks to Lucy's connections to the national archives, they'd managed to get their hands on photos of the patients themselves, including their official records that had been released after the asylum closed its doors. Many of the photos showed despondent-looking men and women in white clothes, their faces thin and gaunt.

As she scanned through the documents, something made her pause. She was looking at a photograph. The woman in it had a severe face and high cheekbones, her hair long and thin, flowing over her shoulders like a shadow. But something about her struck a chord. Like she'd seen her before… The figure in the bedroom. It wasn't easy to match them up, but the tall, gangly limbs and flowing hair matched the shadowy figure she'd seen last night. Part of her was sure this was the woman she'd seen.

Pushing the photo aside, she rummaged through the patient documents to find the matching record.

Sarah Caldrall. That was the name of the patient. She'd been admitted into the psychiatric hospital by her husband due to being 'hysterical' and 'uncontrollable'. Further down in the notes, however, was the patient's own version of events; she denied any of the allegations her husband had made about her, claiming he only admitted her so that he could get her out of the way while he womanised around town. Whoever had noted down this story had scrawled next to it in red pen: delusional, paranoid. Stuck to the back of the patient's file was a photocopied news article. Avery squinted at the small print, scanning through it, and felt herself go cold.

The article reported on the brutal death of Sarah Caldrall that had happened while she was a patient here. One of the other patients who'd been suffering from severe paranoid schizophrenia had believed Sarah to be a spy that had infiltrated the hospital for sinister purposes. She'd made several attempts on Sarah's life during this time, including pushing her down the stairs and sneaking broken glass into her food. And although Sarah had managed to survive those attacks, she was finally killed one night when the patient broke off a metal bar from the end of her bed and used it to beat her to death. Sarah's story was a deeply violent and gruesome one, and she had been wrongfully killed by another seriously mentally-disturbed patient. The staff couldn't have done a very good job of keeping their patients safe if she had access to such weapons, and there was evidence in other records of the experiments and procedures that the doctors there carried out on their patients. Avery felt a shiver of disgust roll over her at the thought of what these people must have suffered at the hands of unmediated medical science.

But if that had been Sarah she'd seen watching Lucy last night, what did she want? Why did her spirit remain here after all these years? Was it the sudden, violent nature of her death and the grief and anger as a result that tethered her here still?

Rising suddenly from her chair, she took the photo of Sarah Caldrall and went to find Caroline.

The psychic looked up when she walked in, her eyes automatically going towards the photograph Avery was holding. "Found who you were looking for?"

Avery bobbed her head, showing her the photo. "Her name's Sarah Caldrall. She was killed by another patient here. I believe this is who I saw last night."

Caroline pursed her lips, staring hard at the photo. "I've seen her here too," she said eventually. "I've felt her anger and her grief at being trapped here. But she's not the only one."

Avery looked at her in question.

"There are so many souls at unrest here. I've never been to a place with so much energy. They're all waiting for some kind of salvation, something to set them free."

"Salvation? Can we give it to them?" Avery asked.

Caroline nodded hesitantly. "We can help them pass over to the other side. Most of them don't want to stay here, but need a little help crossing over. Others… stay for a reason.

But if Sarah wants to move on, then we can help her."

"By performing a séance?"

Caroline nodded again. "In speaking to the spirits that linger here, we can help resolve whatever it is that ties them here, allowing them to move on."

Avery nodded, looking back down at the photo of the woman. She seemed so lost and miserable, her eyes haunting even in shades of black and white. If her story was true, then it was no surprise, given how her husband abandoned her here. If she could, she wanted to help what remained of Sarah Caldrall move on. "I think I'd like to do that. Hold a séance, and help some of the spirits pass on-"

"Woah, woah, wait a second," a voice spoke from behind them, making both women start. Nathan was standing in the doorway of the room, his arms folded across his chest. "We're not allowing *anyone* to pass over yet. Not until we capture enough evidence. If we cross over every spirit, there'll be nothing left to catch on camera. Then what will our viewers think?"

Avery frowned, and Caroline stiffened. "Don't you want to help them?"

"Well yeah," Nathan said impatiently, "but not until we finish our investigation. Okay? No seances until the last day."

He finished with a huff and turned away, leaving Avery scowling after him. She wasn't a fan of his attitude. She knew they were there to investigate the house and get evidence for the podcast, but she wanted to respect the souls that lingered here too. Using them for their own purposes seemed unfair.

Caroline gasped softly, and Avery saw the woman's cheeks pale. "What's the matter?"

She shook her head, her gaze darting around the room. "Nathan shouldn't have said those things. The presence in the room… it has turned angry. Vengeful."

"What?" Avery blurted. "Nathan angered them?"

Caroline nodded. "The whole atmosphere in here has changed. From benign to angry."

Avery gritted her teeth. He knew that messing around with these things could only bring harm to them, especially if the negative energies here were strong enough to manifest.

"Hey guys, ready to get some dinner soon?" Lucy asked, coming in. When she noted the tension in the air, she stopped and looked at Avery and Caroline. “Everything okay?”

“Yeah,” Avery said stiffly. “Let’s go get the others.”

Nathan shook away another spell of dizziness as the five of them sat around the kitchen table, sharing out the lunch Lucy had made them all. He'd been overwhelmed by a feeling of fatigue since leaving the two women in the sitting room, and he couldn't seem to shake it off.

Avery watched him carefully from across the table. After the comment he'd made about not allowing any of the spirits to pass on, Caroline had noted a serious shift in the atmosphere of the house. She wasn't sure if the others could feel it, but she hoped Nathan understood that he shouldn't be so disrespectful towards the spirits at unrest here. They had seen, time and time again, that angry spirits could cause harm if they were strong enough. While they had never experienced a vengeful spirit in any of the houses they'd investigated, it was something they ought to be cautious of.

With a sigh, Avery picked up half of her sandwich and bit into it.

She froze.

Something cracked beneath her teeth, and the taste of blood filled her mouth. Dropping the sandwich to the table, she reached with trembling fingers into her mouth and pulled out a shard of glass, covered in blood. "W-what?!"

"Avery, are you okay?" Lucy asked, watching as her face drained of colour, becoming a sickly shade of grey.

"N-no! What the hell. What's this doing in my food?"

The others stared at her. "Avery, it's just a piece of lettuce."

"Huh?" She looked back down at her hand, where she'd been holding the glass between her fingers. They were right. It wasn't glass at all, but a piece of mangled lettuce.

"I…" she stuttered, her mouth moving uselessly. "Sorry. I'm sorry." She quickly dropped the lettuce, her heart thudding painfully in her chest. What was wrong with her? She'd been convinced there had been glass in her food. Was it because of what she'd read about Sarah Caldrall?

She stood up without a word and went through to the kitchen, running the tap. The sensation of glass in her mouth was still there, and she could still taste blood, even though the water was clear when she rinsed her mouth out.

After drinking two glasses of water, the sensation finally passed, and she felt a little better. She wiped a trembling hand over her mouth.

When she went back into the main room, the others were staring at her. She forced a smile. "Sorry about that guys. I guess I'm more tired than I thought," she said quickly.

Caroline scraped back her chair. Her face had turned a strange pallor, and she clutched her stomach. "I'm sorry, but I don't feel so well. I'm going to lie down in my room for a bit."

Lucy looked between the two women. "Are you both okay?"

Avery nodded. "I'm fine. Caroline, you go and rest," she said, touching the woman's shoulder gently before taking her seat at the table. She pushed the food away, no longer hungry. "I think this house has just made us… a bit out of sorts. I found out who I saw in our room last night."

Lucy's eyes widened, and Avery dug the picture she'd found earlier out of her pockets. "Her name was Sarah," she said, repeating what she'd told Caroline earlier.

"She was murdered by another patient?" Randall repeated, his voice low. "That's horrible."

"Nathan and I caught something earlier as well," he added, leaning forward. "We were in the old operating room upstairs with the thermal camera, and we got a heat signature of a person. We captured him jumping off the balcony."

"A residual suicide?" Lucy said.

"We think so."

"This place really must have a lot of negative energy," she continued. "We've already caught some great stuff on camera. Maybe we should do a live session after lunch, and share what we have."

"Sounds good to me," Randall agreed. "Nathan?"

The three of them turned to Nathan, who was staring intently into space. His head was cocked to the side, as though he was listening to something. "Do you hear that?"

The others went quiet.

In between the silence, Lucy heard the soft murmur of voices.

"I don't hear anything," Randall said, but Lucy shushed him.

"No, I can... I can hear them. Voices," she said. "Like someone's whispering really quickly."

Nathan nodded.

"I think it's coming from the kitchen," she said, biting her lip in concentration. "I can't hear what they're saying."

"Let's go check it out," Randall said, and the other two stood from the table to follow.

As soon as the three of them went through to the kitchen, the whispering stopped.

Randall pulled an EVP recorder out of his pocket, switching it on. "Maybe we'll be able to catch the voices with this," he suggested.

"Hey, where's Nathan?" Lucy asked suddenly, realizing there was one missing from their group.

As the others glanced at each other, something thudded from inside the sitting room.

"Nathan? You alright?" Lucy shouted, pushing open the door between the two rooms and peeking inside. "Nathan!"

He was on the floor on his back, his eyes closed and his chest rising and falling quickly.

"Guys, Nathan's passed out," she said, rushing to his side. She gripped his shoulder and shook it roughly. "Nathan, wake up!"

"What's up with him?"

Avery shook her head. He had been looking clammy and slightly dazed while they'd been sat at the table, but he hadn't said anything about not feeling well.

"Why won't he wake up?" Lucy asked nervously. "Nathan? Nathan, can you hear me…"

Nathan couldn't move.

His body was strapped to a chair, the hard bristles of the shackles cutting into his skin whenever he tried to wriggle against them.

His vision was hazy. A strange fog seemed to cloud the edges of his periphery, making everything seem disproportionate and far away.

He blinked against the encroaching fog, clearing his head.

As things came into focus, he realised he was not alone.

Standing opposite him was a man with an unruly grin. He was short and thin, dressed in a white doctor's coat, and his grey hair was receding from his wide forehead.

"Don't scream now," he said, and Nathan became aware of what the doctor was holding. A pair of pliers glinted wickedly in the lamplight above them, and he flexed away from them before realising he couldn't move.

What was going on? What was the doctor going to do to him?

The man stretched the pliers towards his hand, and he struggled harder against the straps.

"No," Nathan gasped as the doctor gripped one of his fingers and squeezed the head of the pliers around the tip of his fingernail. "No no no no no…"

The doctor's grin stretched unnaturally across his face as he pulled, wriggling the pliers left and right as he attempted to pull his fingernail free from the skin.

"Please stop, oh god," Nathan gasped, squeezing his eyes closed. "Please stop…"

"Nathan? Nathan, can you hear me?"

His eyes fluttered open, his retinas stinging in the sudden glare of light. Three familiar faces hovered above him. "H-huh?"

Lucy blew out a sigh of relief, helping Nathan sit up from the floor.

"What happened?" He said, reaching up to touch the back of his head. He winced at the tenderness of his scalp. He must have hit it against the floor when he fell.

“I don’t know. You fainted,” Randall said. “You alright?”

He blinked, suddenly remembering the dream he’d been having. Only, it had seemed so much more than a dream at the time. It felt real. Far too real, from the doctor’s strange smile to the pain exploding across his fingertips.

He yanked his fingers in front of his face with a gasp, checking that each nail was intact. None of them were missing. And yet he could still feel the horror from the dream, the cold metal of the chair and the shackles around his wrists.

He began to shake, clutching his hands against his chest. Horror dawned on him. Had his dream been some kind of vision? Removing fingernails wasn’t an uncommon practice in places like this. A form of torture that sick doctors performed on their sick patients.

“Hey, Nathan? You alright, man?” Randall said, crouching in front of him.

Nathan flinched back, unable to find his voice. In his head, all he saw was the doctor’s grisly smile, and the pliers coming towards him…

The lights flickered above her, casting momentary intervals of darkness across the room.

Amid the faint buzz of the fluorescents, she could hear someone breathing. It was a heavy, ragged sort of pant, out of sync with her own, coming from somewhere slightly to her left.

When she opened her mouth to speak, she found her tongue a dead weight in her mouth, and a soft whimper slurred out from her attempts. Her throat prickled with dryness, and her lips cracked when she opened them.

The rest of her body felt numb too. Like she was under some sort of anaesthetic, or paralysis. When she tried to move her arms, they wouldn't respond.

"Don't move too much," a voice spoke, breaking up the breathing. It had the same low, raspy quality.

A figure moved into her periphery, and a scream tore silently through her body.

A short, gaunt-looking man smiled thinly at her. In one hand, he held a strange metal implement that was stained in blood. The doctor's coat he was wearing was also heavily smeared in blood. "You don't want to open the stitches."

Caroline jerked out of her dreams with a gasp, overcome by a sudden surge of nausea. Bile filled her mouth, making her cheeks swell, and she untangled herself from the covers with hasty movements, sweat pouring down her back as she stumbled into the adjoining bathroom.

She fell against the floor, her kneecaps cracking on the tiles, and began to retch into the toilet bowl. A small stream of bile gave way to vomit, and the water in the toilet turned a gruesome shade of red. She cried softly, her throat burning as she continued to throw up blood, her knuckles turning white against the ceramic.

What was happening to her?

Her whole body heaved and trembled as she emptied her stomach, sweat running down her skin as her body undulated with fever.

When at last the urge to vomit subsided, Caroline leaned back on her heels and raised her trembling hands to her face. Blood splattered the backs of them, startlingly bright and vivid against the clammy paleness of her skin.

She squeezed her eyes closed, unable to stand the sight of the blood.

In the darkness of her mind, the smell of it only grew stronger, thick and repugnant. Her tongue was coated with blood and bile, and the sickness in her stomach came back.

A quiet sob parted her lips. What was happening to her? She'd never experienced anything like this before, even in her career as a psychic. She had dealt with negative energies before, but none had caused her to be ill like this.

Breathing heavily through her nose, she opened her eyes, and sucked in a sharp breath.

The blood was gone. Her hands were clean, and the vomit in the toilet was not the bright shade of red it had been before, but a sickly brown.

Had she merely imagined the blood? Was it her own mind playing tricks on her… or something else?

Every part of her body trembled as she pushed herself to her feet, flushing the toilet and washing her hands in the sink. She rinsed out her mouth half a dozen times and splashed her face, but her cheeks still hadn't regained their colour and she could still taste blood and bile in her mouth.

Feeling fatigued, she nevertheless went back downstairs to see how the others were getting on. She had to pause mid-way down the stairs as her body began to tingle and she felt suddenly faint, but then the sensation passed, and she made it to the bottom.

The malevolence she had felt earlier after Nathan's comment still lingered in the crevices of the house, but it didn't seem as potent as before, and she breathed a sigh of relief as she went into the sitting room.

Although it was still early, the fire had already been lit, and Caroline found the soft crackle of flames a comforting noise.

The other four were sitting around the hearth in a sullen sort of silence, watching the fire with ruminative expressions.

Then she saw Nathan, and her nausea from earlier began to creep back. “Nathan?”

The others registered her presence, and Lucy went wide-eyed. “Caroline? Are you okay?” She asked, standing to her feet. “You don’t look so good.”

Caroline waved away her concerns, ignoring her own condition as she approached Nathan. She could see it all over his face; the abject terror he felt towards the house. Something must have happened while she was gone. She reached for him and touched her fingers to his shoulder, and her mind burned with images. A doctor’s sly smile, a patient strapped to a chair, the agony in their screams as their fingernails were torn out, one by one.

She pulled away with a gasp. “My god,” she whispered, pressing her trembling fingers to her chest. “You experienced that?”

Nathan tried to back away from her, the fear on his face increasing.

“It’s okay,” she said quickly. “You’re not harmed. That was the spirits showing their anger towards you. They’re telling you that this is *their* house.” She shook her head, strands of hair falling into her eyes. “You’d best not make light of the situation any further, and hopefully they will calm down.”

Nathan nodded, and he looked down at his feet.

“I-I’m sorry. I never meant… it was a foolish thing to do, angering the spirits like that. That’s the number one rule of ghost investigation,” he said.

Caroline nodded. “I’m glad you understand that. I know we’re here to gather evidence, but we must respect the house’s other inhabits too. After all, they’ve been here a lot longer than us.”

Nathan nodded, and the others exchanged looks of mixed relief and confusion.

"Now that we're all back together, shall we do another podcasting session? We have quite a lot to cover."

They all nodded, and even Caroline felt better at the thought of some normalcy.

"I might sit this one out," she said, "but I'll stay in the room with you."

Avery nodded, taking the psychic's arm and helping her into a seat by the fire, out of the camera's view. "Are you sure you're okay?" She whispered.

Caroline smiled grimly. "I'll be fine."

Avery moved away, and Randall began to set up the camera for the session.

"Okay, going live in five minutes. You sure you're feeling up to this, Nathan?"

The man nodded. A little flush of colour had returned to his cheeks, and he allowed a small smile. "Thanks to Caroline, I'm feeling a little better."

Randall nodded, but cast a wary glance towards him. He still hadn't told them exactly what had happened, or what he'd witnessed during his blackout. He'd been too freaked out to even form coherent sentences, but he was glad the psychic had managed to calm him down with her reassurances.

Don't anger the spirits.

"Hey there ghost streamers," Randall started as the live began. "We're coming at you again with a live from the infamous Redburn Manor, formerly known as the Redburn Mental Institute, to investigate the alleged rumours of paranormal activity."

"I think it's safe to say that we're not alone here," Lucy added, nodding. "We've got a lot in store for you today, including new evidence of paranormal activity."

Comments started flooding in on the live chat, ranging from excited fans of the show to sceptics coming on just to call them liars and frauds. They were used to getting comments like that, and tried their best to dismiss them. They didn't have time to try and convince individuals who thought they knew better. All of the evidence they captured was genuine and they shared as much of it as they could with their viewers, asking for opinions and whether anyone could debunk it.

"And we'll be doing a live EVP session on camera," Nathan added, perking up. "How about we get started with that first?"

The others agreed, and Randall picked up the voice recorder.

"We could use dowsing rods too," Avery suggested. "I've been practicing with them, and I think I've gotten a pretty good grasp of it."

"Great," Nathan said, nodding. "Let's try some spirit communication, then."

Randall handed Lucy the camera to film while the others gathered their equipment.

"Caroline? Can you point us in the direction where the energy feels strongest?" Avery whispered to the psychic.

She nodded and closed her eyes, opening herself up to the room. She could usually sense where presences gathered most often, as residual energy collected in those places more strongly than others.

"There. That corner," she said, motioning to the corner by the fireplace. "That's where I felt the energy before too. The one who was watching us."

Avery nodded and directed the others over to the corner. "Our psychic said this is where most of the negative energy is gathered. So we'll try doing an EVP session here first."

Randall cleared his throat, setting the device to record.

"If there's anyone in here with us, we'd like to speak with you. My name's Randall, and I'm here with Lucy, Nathan and Avery. Can you tell us your name?"

They waited for a few moments, letting the device pick up any anomalies of sound that might be a spirit attempting to communicate.

"Were you a patient here, at Redburn Asylum?"

"Did you die here?" Nathan continued, his voice low. "Were you mistreated by the staff?"

They waited in silence again, shuffling their feet as they listened out for anything in the immediate vicinity.

Lucy gasped quietly, drawing the others' attention to her. She turned around, the camera falling sideways in her hands.

"What's wrong?"

"I… don't know. I thought I felt something. It was like a breath, or a whisper, on the back of my neck."

The others stared into the darkened room behind her. "Was that you?" Randall said. "Are you trying to tell us something?"

They waited again, but all was still and quiet.

Avery collected the dowsing rods from her bag while the others continued asking questions. Many still believed that dowsing was a pseudoscience that relied on nothing but coincidence and luck, but she believed otherwise. She'd had success in the past communicating with spirits through them, and she'd been getting better at reading the movements of the rods, gauging what exactly they were trying to tell her. Hopefully they'd work this time too.

She returned to the group, and Lucy panned the camera to her.

Avery forced her lips into a smile. "I'm going to try something known as dowsing," she explained to her viewers. "These two metal rods will help me tap into the energy of the room, and will move in the flow of that energy. I'll ask questions, and use the rods to interpret the energy of the room into answers. It sounds a little strange, but it does work." She nodded at the others and began to relax her body, breathing slowly through her nose. The key was to be relaxed and loose, letting the rods guide her rather than the other way around.

She spread her legs slightly apart, level with her shoulders, and held her arms close to her sides with the rods stretched out in front of her. She cleared her mind, focusing on the questions she wanted to ask, and attuning herself to the rods. For the moment, they remained still.

"Okay, now I need to calibrate them to match the answers. The rod on the left will mean 'No', while the rod on the right will signify 'Yes'. Is that clear? Left is no, right is yes. I'm going to ask some questions now, and the rods will move depending on the answer I'm receiving."

She went quiet then, and began to walk around the room. The rods wavered slightly as she went, and she followed the direction they seemed to be taking her, reading the movement as she had been taught to do. Dowsing wasn't always easy. It took practise to familiarise yourself with what the rods were trying to say.

She turned towards the doorway of the sitting room, and the rods crossed over each other in an 'X' shape.

"The energy is strong here," she said as the rods clinked against each other. "Is there someone here who would like to speak?"

She kept an eye on the rods, trying not to focus on the others watching behind her. She focused only on the question she was asking, watching the rods for any sign of communication.

After a few seconds, the rod on the right began to inch away from the other.

"Is that a yes? You would like to speak?"

The rod wavered, then moved more to the right.

Avery nodded, trying to quell the thrum of excitement in her and concentrate. "Were you a patient here, when the house was a mental institute?" She asked as the rods levelled again.

After a few seconds, the rod on the right began to move again. "Yes," she said out loud. "You were a patient here. Did you die here?"

The rod on the right bobbed again. The one on the left stayed where it was.

"You did," she said sadly. "I'm sorry. It can't have been very nice staying here."

The right rod moved back to the middle, and the left one jerked. "No."

All of a sudden, both of the rods dropped, as though the energy had dispersed.

Then, just as quickly, the rods crossed over again, even more strongly than before. "Huh? Are… are you still there?"

The rods stayed crossed over, then the one on the right began to move again.

"Am I… speaking to the same spirit?"

The one on the left this time. The energy now was much stronger, and the rods moved with sharp, jerky movements. *No*. "A different spirit?" She cleared her throat. "Were you a patient here too?"

The one on the left stayed where it was. "No? Were you here after the Asylum was shut down?"

No again.

"Then… were you a doctor here?"

The rods wavered, then the one on the right jerked. Her arms were beginning to ache. "Yes. You were a doctor?" For some reason, a prickle of dread tiptoed over her neck, and she felt an uncomfortable weight settle in her stomach. "I see. Did you… did you perform lobotomies on the patients here?"

She heard one of the others move behind her, breaking her concentration for a moment.

The rod on the right jerked again. "Yes?" She breathed heavily.

"Did… you die here too?"

The rods fell still.

"Are you still here?"

Again, no answer.

"I think we've lost contact," she said, partly relieved. Speaking with the doctor had drained her.

"That was a great session," Nathan said as they returned to their seats by the fire. It had burned low now, the wood blackened and twisted, but nobody added any more. "Did you get anything from the EVP?"

Randall shook his head, taking off his headphones. "There was a very faint whisper, when Lucy said she felt something behind her, but I can't for the life of me make out what it's saying."

Lucy gestured for the headphones, passing the camera over to Nathan. She listened to the playback in silence.

Eventually she shook her head. "It's too faint. Maybe we could upload it to the website and see what our viewers think."

"Good idea," Randall said. "Right guys. I think that's about it for this live session. If you have any questions or comments, drop them now and we'll answer a few before we finish."

He scrolled through the live chat on the website stream, reading through some of the questions. Then a flood of comments came in at once, saying things that made his whole body go cold.

There's someone stood behind you.

In the doorway!! Look in the doorway!!

Oh my god, I can see a face. They're behind you.

There's something in the doorway behind you.

There's someone there!! Who is it!!

What the hell is that thing?

Randall twisted round in his seat, his eyes darting nervously to the doorway. He squinted into the darkness, where Avery had been conducting her session with the dowsing rods.

There was nothing there that he could see. "I don't see anything," he said, and Nathan frowned, leaning over to read the comments too.

"What? You guys can see something?" He turned to look too, but he could see nothing beyond the darkness. The evening had fallen in quickly, and the room had darkened considerably now that the fire was burning low. A chill breathed across the room.

"I don't see anything. You sure it's not just a camera glare?"

No, there's definitely someone there.

Looks like a man.

He's just staring at you... so creepy!

I'm really creeped out.

"Well, we'll review the footage later and see if we can see it too. I think that's it from us tonight. We'll upload the evidence we've captured onto the website, so make sure you let us know what you think."

"Thanks for tuning in with us!" Lucy said, trying to keep the fatigue out of her voice.

Avery stayed quiet.

"See you next time, ghost streamers!"

They closed off the podcast and the sullen silence from earlier returned.

All five of them felt exhaustion creeping in from the day, and Caroline was not the only one with a pasty hue to her face.

"How are you feeling?" Lucy asked the psychic when she noticed the woman was frowning at the doorway.

"That doctor you were speaking to," she said, ignoring the question. "I didn't like the energy he was giving off. It felt stronger than the others."

Avery frowned. "I felt that too, with the rods. I've never had such strong communication with a spirit. It almost felt like *he* was leading *me*."

Caroline nodded uneasily. "Be careful not to give them power over you."

"Yeah."

"Well, I think I'm ready to head to bed," Lucy said, stifling a yawn. "I know it's still early, but I can barely keep my eyes open."

Avery nodded in agreement. “It’s been a bit of a rough day. I think we should all get some rest. Especially Caroline and Nathan.”

Nathan glanced at her. “Actually, Randall and I are gonna review the footage we got today. But you three head up. We won’t be much longer.”

“Okay. Goodnight you two. Hope you get some sleep,” Avery said as the three women headed upstairs to their rooms.

Randall waved them off and pulled the laptop towards them. “Let’s check the podcast stream, maybe we’ll be able to see what the viewers saw.”

He pulled up the video and rewound it back a few minutes, to the moment when the comments first started coming in about the figure in the doorway. The two of them leaned closer, squinting to see what was happening in the background behind them.

At first they couldn’t see anything. The doorway was doused in shadow and there was no movement beyond the usual undulation of light.

Then Nathan saw it. Materialising from the darkness like a gruesome hallucination.

In the corner of the doorway, staring out at them with pale, hollow eyes, was the face of a man.

Chapter TEN

Caroline tried not to focus on the nausea still turning in her stomach as she laid awake, staring at the shadows on the ceiling. She didn't like the vibe that the house was giving her. Earlier, when she'd been sick, she had been convinced she was throwing up blood. She had seen it, *smelt* it, as though it was really there. The house must have a strong energy if it could give her such realistic hallucinations. And Nathan too – she'd seen part of what he'd experienced, in his vision with the doctor. She'd never encountered such a strong sense of paranormal energy before, especially in the way it had manifested itself to them. This doctor, whoever he was, seemed to be one of the stronger spirits here, and she could sense a malevolence from him. He made her feel ill in a way she'd never experienced before.

Despite her fatigue, Caroline felt strangely awake. The room was cold, and it chilled her through the blankets so that she lay shivering, her breath misting the air in front of her.

The house was unusually quiet. It settled around the room like dust, laying thickly against the carpet and muffling the sounds of the night. As she lay there, she found herself becoming aware of the house's smell. It was strange, and she couldn't quite place it, but it smelled like something dark and unpleasant. Like a cold shadow, or the corner of a room where the sun couldn't reach and damp festered beneath the plaster. The whole house seemed like that. Sunlight could penetrate no farther than the windows, and everything always seemed caked in gloom and dust. A house born in shadow.

The thoughts went round and round in her mind as she stared up at the ceiling, watching the lampshade swing gently in an invisible draught.

Sleep began to itch at her body, but she was reluctant to let it take her. That dream she'd had… she found herself convinced that if she fell asleep now, she would fall right back into the same dream, right where the last one had ended. The doctor standing over her, covered in blood, holding some kind of medical tool.

You don't want to open the stitches.

These dreams… no, these visions, that she and Nathan were having – she knew they were far more than simply their minds conjuring delusions. It was almost as if the house was showing them, fragments of the past, coagulating with the future. It was the house's memory of the evil it contained, and now it was taunting them with it… or warning them. Caroline knew that in these situations, it was always best to leave before things went too far. But Nathan and the others were stubborn, and they wouldn't leave so easily. Not when the investigation was unfinished. They only had to hang on for one more day. It's not like their dreams could hurt them, no matter how unpleasant they were.

As she grew drowsy, struggling to keep her eyes open, Caroline found herself eventually succumbing to a deep, uneasy sleep…

She was awoken some time later by the sound of something thudding against the floorboards outside her room.

Heavy with sleep, she blinked the grogginess from her vision and sat up, staring at the wall opposite her as she listened to the noises.

Thud, thump, thud, thump.

What the hell was going on out there?

It sounded like footsteps, but not soft or lightly trodden. Heavy and thundering, as though someone was running up and down the staircase, their feet thudding against the wooden slats. Was it the boys coming up to bed? But why were they being so loud?

She listened as the footsteps receded, leaving no echo behind save the shuffle of silence falling back into place.

But only a moment later, the footsteps came back again, louder than before. They seemed to stop right outside her room, and she envisioned someone standing on the other side of the door, waiting for her to come out.

Feeling agitated and restless, she got up from the bed and padded silently across the room. She paused at the door, breathing shallowly as she listened to what was happening on the other side.

When she heard nothing, she lowered herself to her knees and pressed her head down to the floor, peering beneath the gap.

There was no silhouette of a person, or a break in the shadows. Nothing to suggest there was anyone out there at all.

Pursing her lips, she climbed back to her feet and gingerly pulled the door ajar, peering through.

There really was nobody out there. She must have been mistaken about hearing the footsteps stop outside her door. She had still been caught in that limbo between sleep and wakefulness when she'd heard them, and it was easy to displace sounds in a house like this.

Nevertheless, that didn't change the fact that she'd heard someone running up here.

Caroline stepped further across the threshold, she twisted her head left and right, straining to see the very end of the corridor. To her left, she could barely make out the silhouette of the staircase. Beyond that, it was too dark to see. The air thickened around her as she breathed heavily through her nose.

"Nathan? Randall? Are you up here?" She whispered, her voice immediately getting swallowed up by the shadows.

When she received no response, she stepped out completely onto the landing, shivering as her bare feet touched the floor.

The air was chilled, and she could feel a draught coming in from somewhere, stirring the hair around her shoulders.

She moved forward through the darkness, reaching out blindly with her hands.

When she reached the top of the stairs, she peered down through the darkness, bringing her brows together.

"Nathan? Randall? You down there?" She said, keeping her voice low for fear of waking the others. She didn't want to cause a disturbance over nothing.

From somewhere downstairs, she heard something knock faintly against the wall. A gentle tap and thud, perhaps of something falling.

Swallowing back the lump in her throat, she began to descend the stairs. Stretching out her hands, her fingers touched the spongy wood of the banister, and she felt a prickling paranoia that a hand was reaching out to touch hers in the dark. She quickly pulled away, clenching her fists against her chest instead, where her heart was thudding dully beneath.

"Guys? Is there someone down here?"

She reached the bottom of the stairs and paused, listening. Pipes gurgled in the kitchen and the wind blew against the chimney, rattling the iron grate, but she heard no voices.

Maybe the boys had already gone to bed after all.

So who had she heard on the stairs?

Walking on her tiptoes, she approached the door to the sitting room. Her fingers brushed the handle, and it opened with a soft groan.

It was dark inside. The fire was out, and there was only a faint tincture of smoke lingering in the room. It was cold too. The fire must have gone out a while ago.

Caroline turned away, deciding there was nobody down here after all, when something rustled across the back of her neck.

She went still, her shoulders tensing up.

Someone whispered behind her. It was a female voice, speaking faintly but somewhere close to her ear. Close enough for her to feel the mild rustle of air from their breath.

"Is someone here?" She asked, returning her gaze to the room. She stepped inside this time, unseeing in the darkness as she used her natural senses to guide her forward. "Did someone say something just now?"

There was movement in the dark, a blur of shadow to her left. She turned quickly, her eyes searching the room, but she saw nothing beyond that impenetrable gloom.

Then she felt it. Something in the corner of the room, watching her from the dark. Invisible eyes prickling over her.

She felt a shiver of discomfort, gooseflesh spreading along her skin, and wrapped her arms close around her body.

"Is there someone here?" She asked again, staring at the corner by the fireplace, feeling the energy gather there as the shadows thickened. It was the same presence she had felt the same day they had arrived, watching them from the corner of the room. Even now, she couldn't read the entity's intentions. She didn't know what it wanted from them or why it was there.

She went to speak again, then stopped herself.

Her hands tightened into fists.

Part of her knew it wasn't a good idea to reach out like this. Not while she was alone, not while she was vulnerable in the dark. If she initiated contact, she had no idea what the entity might do.

Instead, she feigned ignorance, dragging her gaze away from the shadows as though she had felt nothing there.

Fighting the urge to look behind her, the psychic slowly retreated from the room, trying not to appear too harried.

Mid-way up the stairs, she flicked a momentary glance over her shoulder. Her eyes brushed past the mirror hanging in the hallway, and for a second, she saw something staring back.

Then she fumbled up the rest of the stairs, hurrying to her room, and collapsed with her back against the door.

It was going to be a long night.

The breakfast table was strangely subdued the following morning. Everyone seemed laden down with fatigue from the day before, unable to lift their eyes from their laps as they munched unenthusiastically on their food.

"So, what's the plan of action today?" Lucy eventually asked, trying to keep her voice cheerful. Her smile fell short of reaching her eyes, lingering awkwardly on her face.

"I think I'd like to take a look at some of the other rooms," Avery said first, lifting her eyes from her cereal bowl to glance at the faces around her. "We haven't explored the whole house yet, so it might be good to do a few more EVP sessions in places we haven't investigated."

"I'll join you for that," Caroline said, sipping at a glass of water. She cleared her throat. “There are rooms I would like to investigate more too.”

“Are you sure you’re feeling up to it?” Lucy asked kindly. There were dark shadows beneath the psychic’s eyes from her unrested sleep, but she nodded anyway.

“I’m feeling a lot better than yesterday. And there’s no harm in a few EVP sessions.”

Lucy spooned some cereal into her mouth and nodded. “I think I’ll join you as well then,” she said between mouthfuls. “I want to take a look at the old operating room. Nathan and Randall said they caught something in there, right?”

The boys nodded across the table. “We got a residual suicide through the thermal camera. Oh, and we forgot to show you last night, but we caught something on the livestream. It looks like a figure watching us from the doorway.”

They pulled up the image and zoomed in to show the others. Avery supressed a shudder at the visage of a man’s face staring out at them from the dark.

“That’s pretty creepy,” she said. They’d never caught a face on camera before, never mind in the middle of a livestream.

"Looks like he's wearing some kind of coat. A doctor, perhaps?" Lucy suggested, squinting at the hazy image.

"That's what we thought. Maybe the doctor Avery was speaking to last night."

She nodded silently, looking away from the image.

Nathan himself shuffled in discomfort, and Caroline wondered if he was remembering the doctor from his vision. She'd only had a brief glimpse herself, but she remembered his cruel smile.

"While you three are exploring the house," Randall continued, oblivious to his friend's discomfort, "we're gonna stay down here and keep reviewing footage. There's a ton we haven't gone through yet, and there's some EVPs I'd like to listen back to as well."

"Sounds good. Call us if you find anything interesting," Lucy said as they stacked up their breakfast pots and got their equipment ready.

Randall cocked his chin. "Likewise."

Lucy switched on her camera and gestured towards the door separating the kitchen from the sitting room. "Want to head through to the main room first? We had a pretty good EVP session in there last night. We might get some more voices."

"Good idea."

The three girls moved into the sitting room, which seemed drab and gloomy with the curtains closed and the fire unlit. There wasn't a lot of natural light coming through anywhere, and it felt like the house had been trapped in shadow since they got there. It was no wonder the hotel and breakfast hadn't lasted very long.

"Okay, we're recording," Lucy said, holding out the EVP device towards the room.

"Is there anyone here who would like to speak with us?" Avery started, leading the questions. "We'd like to talk with you, if you'd let us."

They stayed quiet for a few minutes, looking around the room.

"Is the patient from yesterday still here?" She continued, hoping the doctor wasn't around instead. "We didn't finish our conversation."

Caroline asked a few more questions about the Asylum and what it was like back then, and they played back the recording to see if they caught any voices.

"There, I hear something!" Lucy blurted as the audio crackled slightly and a voice that belonged to none of them came through. "I'll play it back." She rewound the tape again and held it closer to their ears.

In the muffled silence, a voice spoke in broken words.

"*The lady… is… unwell.*"

Avery blinked, looking up at the other two. "The lady is unwell? Is that what she's saying?"

Lucy nodded. "That's what I can hear." She pursed her lips, playing it once more. "It sounds like a little girl's voice."

Caroline agreed. "That's what I'm hearing as well."

"Do you think she's talking about one of the patients?" Lucy asked, her brows coming together as she listened to the audio once more. The child's voice embedded in the static.

"Maybe," Caroline said, feeling her stomach twist. *Or one of us*.

The rest of the audio had nothing else unusual, so they tried again, staying where they were in the corner of the room.

"The girl that just spoke, are you still here? Who is unwell?"

"Is someone sick? Are *you* unwell?"

"Can you tell us your name?"

They waited a few minutes, then played it back again.

After the first question, they heard what sounded like a quiet sob, or a laugh. It was difficult to tell against the crackly feedback, but it didn't sound the like the child anymore.

Then, a few moments later, another voice.

"*Must leave. Die later*."

The words here were clearer, coming through the static like a disembodied echo that made all of them shiver.

"Is she telling *us* to leave?" Lucy asked, her voice gentle even as the lines on her face creased.

Caroline said nothing. *Must leave. Die later.* Was she speaking about the past or the present? Was it another patient she was warning, or one of them?

"Let's move to a different room," Avery suggested. "I'm not liking the feeling in here."

The others agreed, and they went across the hallway to what appeared to be a study; perhaps the manager's office, back when the place was a functioning Bed and Breakfast. "This hasn't changed too much from the original, I don't think," Lucy said as she flipped through the house's plans that she'd brought with her. "This was a doctor's office back in the 1940s. Someone died in here, while they were undergoing some treatment. I guess it served as an operating room too."

Caroline shuddered as a cold spot touched the back of her neck. She could feel the air shift around her, feeling heavy and thick with negative energy.

"I don't like this room," she said quietly. "Something bad happened here."

The others stared at her, as though waiting for an explanation, but she couldn't give them one. All of a sudden, she could see it happening. She closed her eyes, stumbling back to lean against the desk, and saw the room not as the study it was now, but as it was back in the Asylum. Strange implements and devices were littered along the table, blood-stained gloves and rusted shackles. And a figure, standing in the corner of the room, watching them with a wolfish grin. The doctor.

"Caroline?"

She opened her eyes, and the vision passed. Avery and Lucy watched her with concern.

"I'm fine," she said.

Lucy stepped back. "We caught something on the EVP," she said. "Listen." She played the recording for the psychic, watching her closely.

There was a short, sharp cry of pain, and someone's voice saying "Catch you" in a low, grating whisper.

Caroline winced at the cry. Expressions of fear or pain were not uncommon in EVPs, but it always gave her a chill to think these spirits still experienced those cruel moments before their death.

"Let's finish up in here," Avery suggested, seeing Caroline's expression.

Lucy gave the room a final, lingering glance, a shadow appearing between her brows, before following the others.

They went up to the first floor next, where the guest bedrooms were. “This is where the patients would have stayed. Back then, these were more like closets, but the hotel renovators knocked through to expand the rooms,” Lucy explained as they piled into one of the bedrooms.

She looked back down at her notes. “I’m not quite sure which patients stayed in this room, but I have it written down in my notes that several passed away in their sleep, either due to medical negligence or as a result of self-inflicted wounds. The staff here didn’t make the place very safe for the patients,” she added sadly. “A lot of asylums were unregulated and safety measures were never properly implemented.”

Avery thought about Sarah Caldrall and the patient who killed her. She was sure that, had the staff not been so careless about giving patients access to glass and possible weapons, the woman might have lived.

“I’m not feeling much here,” Caroline said as she circled the room, reading the energies that lingered. “I don’t feel much energy. I don’t think any spirits are attracted to this place.”

“Shall we try the next room?”

"Sure."

Randall hit pause on the laptop, his eyes wide as he stared at the screen displaying the audio monitor. "I've got something," he said to Nathan, tapping him on the shoulder when he didn't respond.

Nathan quickly pulled off his headphones, turning to Randall quizzically. "What's up?"

"Listen to this."

He handed over the headphones he'd been using, rewinding the clip for Nathan to listen to.

Nathan held his breath as Randall hit play, listening hard to the noise beyond the faint hiss and crackle of static.

At first, he couldn't hear much. But then something interrupted the flow of the static; the ragged hiss and gasp of someone breathing. It was a heavy, undulating sort of sound, as though someone was breathing erratically in excitement or fear. As the breathing moved away, a faint voice whispered the word 'no'. Nathan frowned, straining to hear what was happening. The sound of running footsteps grew closer, and a second later something thudded loudly against the floor. A short, sharp wail of someone crying out in pain was the last sound on the clip before everything went quiet.

The silence that followed was heavier than before. Nathan gestured for Randall to play it again, listening intently. He'd never heard such a clear enactment of paranormal activity through an EVP. They hadn't just captured voices, but the sound of movement too.

"That's not the only thing," Randall continued as Nathan tugged the headphones off in mingled awe and horror. "We caught the exact same thing on the thermal cameras too. Watch. The figure on the screen lines up with what we can hear in the audio."

He played the video clip back, and Nathan's face turned a sickly hue as he watched. On the screen, the heat signature of a person was clearly visible. He was on the floor, crawling on his hands and knees, dragging his body forward as though he was hurt. When the footsteps played in the clip, the figure rolled onto his back and threw up his hands as though to defend himself from something. After the scream, the heat signature disappeared completely.

"No way," Nathan breathed. "You think we caught some kind of residual haunting – like the suicide upstairs."

"Maybe," Randall agreed. "Only this one looks like they were being murdered or tortured by someone."

"Shit. This place is really messed up."

Chapter FOURTEEN

Lucy felt a shiver of unease crawl along the back of her neck when she went into the room with the balcony. Nathan had said they'd picked up a heat signature of someone in here committing suicide, and she wondered if they might capture the voice of the victim himself.

Avery and Caroline came in behind her, taking in the room's features, and she went closer to the balcony with the EVP device.

"Is there someone here who would like to speak with us?" She asked, scanning her eyes over the room as though she might be able to feel its presence.

Avery stood behind her, flipping through the records that Lucy had handed her. "A patient named Thomas Stone died here," she said, scanning through the notes. "He killed himself by throwing himself off the balcony."

"That's what Nathan and Randall must have caught on camera," Lucy said. "Is Thomas here? He used to live in this room, according to our records."

She went around the room, touching the walls and the bed frame, trying to connect with some of the energy lingering here. She didn't really know what she was doing, but every now and then, she would feel a tingle run along her fingertips, as though she could sense something there.

"You were a patient here, weren't you? What was it like living here?"

She swallowed back a lump in her throat. Something about the room put her on edge, but she couldn't say what.

"Did the doctors mistreat you?"

She waited a few more minutes, then played the recording back. She held it close to her ear, trying to discern any voices among the static feedback, but she heard nothing out of the ordinary.

Caroline was standing at the balcony doors, staring out at the grey sky, burgeoning with rain. The weather had been gloomy since they'd arrived at the house, creating an endless chill through its rooms.

Leaving Avery flipping through the records, she went to stand beside the psychic.

"How long have you had it?" Caroline said suddenly, making Lucy turn to her in bewilderment.

"Sorry?"

"Your gift. How long have you had it?" She repeated without facing her. Her eyes were trained on the horizon, where a flock of birds were fighting against the wind. "I wasn't sure at first, but I can see it now. You're a sensitive, aren't you?"

"I-I'm not sure what-"

"You're sensitive to certain things," Caroline continued, unfazed. "Haven't you realized? You have a broader reach than most when it comes to the paranormal. You can feel things others can't. Sometimes it draws spirits to you."

Lucy frowned. "I… I don't know," she said. She'd never thought about it before.

"You've seen things that others can't. That others won't believe."

Lucy stared down at her feet, pulling her brows tighter together. "When I was younger," she began uncertainly, "I always used to think that someone was watching me from my closet. Every night, I would feel something in there, just… watching me. At the time, I just shrugged it off as a child's fear though."

"But it wasn't, was it?" Caroline prompted, and Lucy turned to her, her eyes searching.

"What do you mean?"

"The man in the closet. You knew who it was," she continued, and Lucy felt her stomach turn. "It was your Uncle, wasn't it? The one who killed himself."

Lucy looked away, her skin flushing. "Maybe."

"But you were the only one who could feel him there," the psychic continued. "You are sensitive. Even if it's not been as obvious in your life, it's what drew you to the paranormal in the first place."

Lucy said nothing, staring down at her feet. Had Caroline read all of that from her?

Avery stood a short distance away, listening with undisguised awe. She'd known Lucy a few years, but she'd never realised she was what Caroline called a 'sensitive'; someone more in tune with spiritual energies. Sure she'd always had a knack for speaking to spirits in a way that drew them out of hiding, but she'd assumed that was because of the extensive research she often did into the cases they looked at.

The voice recorder in Lucy's hand suddenly began to hiss and crackle, drawing all three women's attention towards it.

"Huh? What's wrong with it?" She muttered, shaking the device as though it would somehow clear up the white noise. The static spat and hissed, as though the whole thing was malfunctioning, and she hit it against the palm of her hand, trying to fix it.

"What's it doing?" Avery asked, and Lucy stepped away from the balcony, wondering if something outside was interfering with it.

With Avery and Lucy's attention on the recorder, neither of them noticed Caroline standing behind them.

She gasped softly and her whole body went motionless, her eyes clouding over with an unnatural haze. Her head snapped back suddenly, her joints creaking, and her body began to jerk this way and that, like she was having some kind of seizure.

Her fingers flexed and cracked and her arms twisted forward, as though she was being manipulated by invisible strings.

She grunted quietly, a strange, animalistic noise, and Lucy glanced behind her. Her eyes went wide. "C-Caroline?" She stammered. "What's wrong? What are you doing?"

The psychic didn't answer. Her lips had gone slack, and a rivulet of drool trickled down her chin.

Then her head twitched forward, her eyes rolling up, and she stared at the two women with white, pupil-less eyes.

Avery grabbed Lucy's arm tightly, pulling her back towards the doorway of the room. "Something's wrong with her," she whispered as Caroline's body began to shudder, and her lips curled up into a strange, distorted smile.

Lucy swallowed, and Avery's nails dug deeper into her arm.

"Caroline?" She whispered, hoping the psychic would hear her. "Caroline, can you hear me?"

The psychic's body jerked forward, and her lips snarled open. "Clink, clink, clink," she said in a voice that was not her own. It was a man's voice, low and hollow. "Clink, clink, clink."

She began to move forward, her hips swinging jerkily and her toes twisting inwards, as though she'd forgotten how to walk properly.

Avery whimpered softly as her back hit the wall. The door was slightly to their left, but neither women were ready to run. Caroline kept coming closer, her milky white eyes staring at them with unnatural clarity. "Clink, clink, clink… and… you're gone."

A low, distressed wail cut across the room, and Lucy and Avery twisted towards the balcony, where it seemed to be coming from.

The cry died out, and they heard a distant thud that made their bodies go cold.

When they turned back to Caroline, she was still staring at them, but her eyes were back to normal, and she blinked at them, disconcerted.

"W-what just happened?" She gasped, reaching up to touch her head.

Avery darted forward as Caroline's legs suddenly gave way and she slumped forward with a soft groan. The psychic took a moment to recollect herself, reaching out to the wall to support her weight.

"Caroline? Are you okay?" Lucy asked, chewing nervously on her lip as the woman pressed her hands to her temples again, squinting her eyes in pain.

"I… I think something jumped me," she said, her voice tumbling out in ragged gasps. "A spirit entered my body without permission. It… it was strange. Like something else was controlling me from the inside."

Lucy's eyes went wide, her lips parting. "Can it do that?"

Caroline nodded weakly. "If a spirit's strong enough, then yes."

"But are you okay now?" Avery asked, gently touching the psychic's shoulder.

"I think so. I'll be fine with a little rest," she assured them, but Lucy remained unconvinced as the psychic winced again, touching the tender skin on her head. "Did I say anything, while…" she trailed off, swallowing.

Lucy nodded. "The device was recording the whole time. Something must have interfered with the frequency."

She played back the audio, skipping over the part where the device had reacted to whatever was in the atmosphere.

"Caroline?" Lucy's voice echoed through the recording, distorted by the feedback so that it sounded strange and unfamiliar. “Caroline, can you hear me?”

Then that low, guttural voice, saying: “Clink, clink, clink…”

Caroline listened to it with increasing discomfort. That wasn’t her voice, and yet she had been the one speaking. Something had used her body as a puppet, robbed her of control. And now she felt violated and wrong, as though her skin was not her own.

Lucy cut off the recording and put the device away. “Maybe we should stop exploring for now,” she said gently.

Caroline nodded. “I… I think I’m going to go and rest for a bit,” she whispered, barely sparing the others a glance as she stumbled out of the room, cradling her hands around her body.

Avery and Lucy stared after her.

“Do you think she’ll be okay?” Avery asked, worrying at her lip.

“Yeah. With some rest, I’m sure she will be,” Lucy said, though she couldn’t disguise her own worry for the woman. She couldn’t imagine what it must be like to have another person enter your body, taking control without your permission, violating every privacy of the human condition.

"Did you hear that scream before?" Avery asked suddenly, turning to the balcony. "Who do you think it was?"

"Most likely it was Thomas, our jumper," she said, and the two of them went over to the doors, throwing them open. A fierce wind gusted through, blowing their hair out behind them.

As they peered over the edge of the railings, they glimpsed what seemed to be an indentation in the bushes below, as though something heavy had fallen on top of it.

But there was nobody there.

Randall stepped out of the bathroom, wiping his hands absently on his trousers as he hummed quietly to himself. He'd bumped into Caroline while on his way upstairs, and she had seemed flustered and anxious about something, barely noticing him as she went passed. He'd tried calling out to her, but she either didn't hear him or had ignored him on purpose.

She'd disappeared into her room before he could catch up with her, and he'd thought it best to leave her alone. If something had happened, he was sure she'd tell them later.

As he was heading back towards the stairs, something made him pause.

Above him, the floorboards shuddered faintly, and a cloud of dust drifted down onto his face. He coughed it away, brushing the plaster from his hair as he stared up at the ceiling.

Was someone up there?

They'd yet to go up to the second floor of the mansion, as their records suggested there wasn't much of interest up there other than a few more bedrooms that had once served as the nurse's quarters. No death or tragedy to speak of.

He drew his brows together, and after a split-second decision, headed towards the staircase that led up to the second floor. It was tucked away on the other side of the corridor, and the smell of dust and damp seemed especially strong as he began climbing the stairs. When he reached out to touch the bannister, it was cold enough to make him flinch, and he instead used the wall to guide him up into the second-floor gloom.

Once he was up there, he took stock of his surroundings. Like the floor below, it stretched out into a long corridor, with doors either side leading to more guest bedrooms of the old bed and breakfast.

A beam of watery sunlight seeped beneath one of the doors, which hung partially ajar, but other than that, the whole corridor was basked in gloom.

Randall hesitated, wondering if he should go back downstairs – Nathan would be wondering where he was by now.

But then he shook away his trepidation and reached for the EVP device he kept in his pocket.

"Might as well see if there's anything interesting up here," he murmured to himself. He started in the room with the open door, poking it open with the tips of his fingers.

It was warmer inside than the rest of the house. The curtains were open and a faint misty glow warmed the air.

"Well, this isn't so bad," he muttered with a weak smile. "Not the kind of place ghosts want to hang out, though."

Stepping further inside, he ran a finger absently over the dresser, smearing dust. He wrinkled his nose in response as it tickled his sinuses.

"Is there anyone up here?" He asked.

A second later, the floorboard groaned again outside the room, making him snap his head towards the open doorway. "Hello? Nathan? Lucy?"

Nobody answered, and when he poked his head through the doorway, he found himself still alone up there.

With a shrug, he left the room behind and went out into the chilly corridor, turning his head left to right as he looked for any signs that suggested he wasn't alone after all.

As he moved towards the next room, he heard someone laugh close by. It was more like a child's giggle, but it sounded strange in the dark, oddly misplaced.

He froze, one foot stretched out in front of him. "Hello?" He said, his voice echoing dully. "Someone up here?"

Another giggle. This one came from the room to his left. With cautious movements, he stepped closer to the door and pressed his ear against the wood.

He couldn't hear anyone inside, but he was sure that's where he'd heard the laughter come from.

Swallowing back his apprehension, he reached for the handle. The mechanism seemed a little rusty, and he had to give it a good shove before it opened.

Once inside, he felt a wave of nausea peel over him.

The smell of damp and mildew was strong enough to make his eyes water, and he held the sleeve of his jumper over his nose to quell the stench. The room must not have been opened in years, let to rot and fester in the cold. Patches of mould had seeped through the plaster, mottling the walls like dark bruises on skin. When he flicked a glance up to the lampshade, he saw husks of dead insects inside the bulb.

There was a small dresser, a mirror sitting on top with its gilt frame rusted and the glass spiderwebbed with hundreds of small cracks, and a double bed with plain sheets. In one corner of the room, closest to the window, the floorboards had been pulled up, exposing wire mesh and underfloor pipes that were old and rusted.

Nobody else was in there.

He glanced down at his EVP, realizing it was crackling faintly with some kind of interference. He frowned, pulling it closer to his ear, trying to figure out what was wrong with it. It never usually emitted feedback like this.

He switched it off and back on again, tapping it against his palms a few times in case the batteries had gotten dislodged inside. Then he held it back to his ear, frowning.

This time, amongst the crackle of noise, a voice hissed back to him.

"Behind you."

He spun round, just as the door swung closed, slamming into place with a dull rattle of hinges.

He flinched back with a yell, his eyes going wide in their sockets. "The hell?" He muttered, reaching for the door handle. But when he tried it, it wouldn't open.

The lock had jammed.

Furrowing his brows, Randall tried both hands, laying them against the handle and giving them a hefty tug. The door shuddered but did not give way. He bit out a frustrated cry and kept trying, hoping the mechanism was rusted enough that it might break if he put enough pressure on it.

Then someone giggled behind him, and his body seized with a cold, prickling dread.

He wasn't alone in here.

Every hair on Randall's arms stood on end as he turned around, a deliberate slowness to his movements.

There was nobody behind him, but he could feel wasn't alone. In the shadows around the room, he felt something watching him.

"What do you want?" He said, his voice choked with fear.

Something shuffled in the dark. He heard

the chafing of movement against the wall to his left. He tried to track it, but he could see nothing. Then the room visibly darkened, and he flicked a glance towards the curtains, his heart stalling in his chest.

The silhouette of a figure was discernible beneath the fabric, blocking out the grimy light that had been coming through before.

Was there someone stood there?

Randall clenched his hands, feeling sweat accumulate against his palms.

"Hello?" He said, his voice coming out in a strangled whisper. He tried to step forward, but his body wouldn't move. Part of him was screaming not to check behind the curtains, afraid of what he would see.

You're a paranormal investigator, he chastised himself. *You're not supposed to run away.*

Swallowing back the lump in his throat, he forced his body to move forward, reaching out to the curtains. His fingers grasped the fabric, and his heart slowed in his chest as he pulled it aside, unearthing the window beneath.

He felt a gust of air brush past him, and the curtains fell slack.

There was nobody there.

Something clicked behind him, and he breathed a heavy sigh of relief as the door swung open on a gentle breeze. Whatever presence had been taunting him seemed to have gone, and the air felt physically lighter, as though it had been burdened before by that unnatural energy.

Wiping away the sweat that had gathered on his brow during those few tense minutes, he switched off his EVP – no longer throwing out static interference – and put it away.

Nathan would be waiting for him, and Randall wasn't sure he wanted to stay up there much longer on his own. He wasn't sure what kind of spirit he had encountered, but it seemed to have enjoyed playing with him and his fear, and that unsettled him. There was usually a more malicious intent behind entities who taunted people like that.

He hurried out of the room, throwing one last lingering glance over his shoulder, then went back downstairs.

When Randall rushed into the kitchen, eager to tell Nathan about his experience, the first thing he saw was his friend's body, sprawled out on the floor beside the table. His eyes were closed, fluttering beneath the lids, and his breathing sounded wheezy and strained.

"Nathan?" Randall gasped, crouching next to him and shaking his shoulders desperately. "Nathan? Wake up! Nathan?"

Nathan walked down the dimly lit hallway, the shackles around his hands clinking with each movement. Laughter cackled unbidden from his mouth, shrill and hysterical.

“See, this is why we need to do this, Charles,” a voice bellowed behind him, making him laugh harder in response. He didn’t turn around, but he knew it was the doctor who was speaking.

The pressure of a hand touched the back of his neck and pushed him forward, deeper into the gloom.

“You’ve given us no choice.”

Nathan kept laughing, his throat and lungs burning as the noise tore through him. He wanted to stop, but his body continued to convulse with hysteria, and he could feel his vocal cords straining with the pressure.

He was pushed into one of the operating rooms upstairs; in the brief glance he gave it, he took in a metal cabinet against one wall, and the gurney that sat in the middle of the room, a bright spot lamp arching over it. The metal looked rusted, caking in reddish-brown stains.

Nathan kept laughing, even as his voice began to crack and rasp.

The doctor behind him guided him onto the gurney, pushing him back so that his head touched the cold fabric of the seat. The short, bony man produced a clamp from his pocket and brought it towards Nathan's mouth, grinning wickedly. "In situations like this, there is no other way to handle it, Charles. It must be done."

As Nathan's jaw opened to laugh, the doctor stuck his fingers into his mouth and grabbed hold of his tongue. Nathan continued to laugh around the doctor's fingers, full of manic hysteria, even as his panicked heartbeat thundered in his ears. The doctor placed the clamp tightly around Nathan's tongue, the cold metal stinging, and Nathan began to struggle. At some point, restraints had been placed around his ankles and wrists, pinning him down onto the gurney.

He writhed and kicked, trying to get free as the laughter continued to pour uncontrollably out of his mouth, his whole body aching with the strain.

Stepping away from the gurney, the doctor went over to the cabinet and retrieved a metal implement from inside, turning back to face Nathan with that sly grin.

When Nathan saw what he was holding, his laughter turned to screams.

"Nathan! Nathan, wake up," Randall croaked, shaking his friend's shoulder vigorously. Sweat was beading along his brow, dripping down into his eyes as they fluttered restlessly with whatever vision he was having.

Without warning, Nathan's eyes flew open and he jolted upright, gasping for breath. His whole body was shaking as he subconsciously reached up and touched his lips. "R-Randall?" He said, his voice sounding oddly strained.

"There you are," Randall said, leaning back against the table leg. "Man, you're really starting to scare me with all this blackout business."

Nathan breathed heavily for a few minutes, trying to reorientate himself.

He was on the floor in the kitchen, where he had been looking over the footage while Randall went to the restroom. Just before he'd blacked out, he'd been staring at the photo of the man in the shadows behind them; the doctor. Was it the same one from his dreams? For some reason, whenever he went to reach for the memory, it slipped between his grasp. As he tried to conjure an image of the doctor, all he could see was that horrible, sickly grin.

"Man, this house is insane," Nathan said, rubbing his eyes.

"No kidding," Randall said, letting out a shaky breath. "I got trapped in a room upstairs."

Nathan looked at him with a start. "What?"

Randall shook his head, pushing hair out of his eyes. "It doesn't matter now. You are okay, right?"

Nathan nodded, parting his mouth to speak just as footsteps thundered out in the hallway.

Avery and Lucy came in together, looking flustered.

"Is everything okay in here? We heard Randall shouting."

Their gazes fell on Nathan, still lying on the floor, his face a strange shade of grey, and they rushed over to him.

Lucy dropped to her knees beside him, Avery behind her. "Nathan! Are you okay? Did you black out again?"

He nodded wordlessly. His tongue still felt strange and heavy in his mouth, and he was reluctant to explain his visions to them. It was bad enough having to experience them once, and he didn't want to upset them any more than he had to by telling them what he saw.

"Something's seriously wrong with this place," Randall muttered, raking a hand through his hair again. "I think-"

Before he could finish, the door to the room slammed open again, bouncing off the wall inside.

Caroline stood in the doorway, framed by the lingering shadows of the afternoon.

"Caroline?" Lucy blurted. "I thought you were resting."

"We need to do a séance," she said without preamble, coming into the room. She wrung her hands together nervously, her eyes darting around the kitchen as she looked for her bags.

"Right now?"

Caroline nodded. “There’s no time to waste,” she muttered, her gaze landing on her bags, tucked beneath the kitchen table. She hauled them out, her hair tumbling down into her face, her wide eyes giving her countenance a manic impression.

“What’s gotten into her?” Randall muttered as she clutched her bag to her chest and stumbled back towards the door.

“Meet me in the study,” was all she said before hurrying out again, a strange urgency to her steps.

The rest of them exchanged uneasy looks. They’d never seen the psychic like this before, and something about the desperation of her voice spooked them. Had something happened?

“We’d better go,” Lucy said, helping Nathan to his feet.

Avery and Randall followed, heading towards the old doctor’s office at the end of the hallway.

It was already dark inside. Caroline had drawn all of the curtains, and the sloping contours of the room made the shadows seem thicker than usual. The psychic was lighting some candles she’d placed on the table, the flames guttering softly in the breeze they carried through.

“Everyone sit down,” she instructed without looking at them, blowing out the match. A faint swirl of smoke blossomed out from the extinguished flame.

They did as she said without question, sitting at each corner of the desk. All of the papers and books that had been scattered on top of it had now been haphazardly thrown onto the floor. The whole study was in disarray.

“Caroline, what’s going on?”

The psychic joined them at the table, her face ghastly in the flickering candlelight. “We need to call to the spirits in the house and banish the one that jumped into my body. There’s a malevolent spirit here, and we need to pass it over before the activity escalates any further.”

The others look at each other, their pale eyes glistening in the dark. “A malevolent spirit?”

She nodded. “More than one,” she added. “At first I thought it was just the doctor,” she said, “but there are others too. The negative energy here is strong, and we need to cleanse some of it before it takes its toll on us.”

The four of them fell silent at her words, and Caroline closed her eyes, stretching out her hands for Randall and Lucy to take hold of. Once they were all linked around the table, the psychic began calling to the spirits of the house.

In the silence that followed, Avery became aware of every shuffle and creak of movement in the house, from the floorboards settling to the wind moaning against the bricks outside and the ragged breathing of the others in the room. She shuffled her feet, trying to block out any distractions and focus. Caroline knew what she was doing. They just had to trust her.

"I'm reaching out to the spirits in this house," Caroline said, her voice crisp and loud in the silence. "If there's one here with us now, please come forward."

They waited in silence. Avery's palms grew sweaty, and she felt her skin flush with anticipation. She fought the urge the fidget, not wanting to disturb the stillness of the room.

"If there are spirits here, I'm calling on you now," Caroline repeated, her voice growing tight with impatience. "Show yourself to us."

Something scraped against the wall on their left, and Avery's eyes flew open. The candle in front of her sputtered again, throwing shadows into sharp relief.

She turned her head, staring at the wall. She could hear something scratching against it… like fingernails.

"What is it?" Lucy whispered.

"I… can't see anything," Nathan said.

Randall pulled his hand away from Avery's and reached for one of the candles, holding it out toward the wall.

The flame guttered, and Avery's throat clenched up.

On the wall, written in bloody fingernail scratches, were the words *clink clink*. The same words that Caroline had spoken when something had taken control of her body. Was the same spirit with them now?

Something clattered faintly against the floor, and Randall lowered the candleflame to see what it was.

A single bloody fingernail lay on the ground.

A visible shudder went through Avery, and every hair on her neck stood up.

"Who is here?" Caroline continued. Her eyes remained closed, her breathing growing shallow as the air in the room turned heavy. "Show yourself."

Across the table from Avery, Nathan breathed heavily through his nose. Every instinct in his body was telling him to run away, that there was something in the room with them, but he held himself in place. He couldn't break the circle, or he risked letting the spirits have power over them.

He flinched suddenly as something brushed against his nose. Something light and thin was tickling him, like a spiderweb, or an insect's spindly legs.

His eyes flew open out of compulsion, and he tipped his head back to see what it was.

A face hung over him. Hollow-eyed and gaunt, with peeling grey skin and long black hair that dangled over him, tickling his forehead and nose. The woman's lips peeled back into an unnaturally long smile that stretched up to her cheekbones, and a scream ripped loose from Nathan's mouth.

The entity above him let out a fiendish roar that shattered the room, blowing out one of the candles in front of him.

Avery screamed when she saw the thing standing behind Nathan, yanking her hands free from the circle and stumbling to her feet.

Lucy followed her, grating back her chair and staring in abject horror at the girl with no eyes.

The two women raced out of the room, extinguishing the rest of the candles as they went so that the room darkened further, shadows encroaching from every direction.

Randall stood shakily to his feet, backing away from the table without taking his eyes off the woman. "Nathan. Get the hell away from there," he hissed as Nathan sat frozen in place, the entity staring down at him with that crooked smile.

His eyes flickered across to Caroline, but she seemed to be in some kind of psychic trance, her lips open and her head slack, completely oblivious to what was happening around her.

Nathan's whole body shook as he tentatively lowered himself off the chair, crawling on his hands and knees beneath the table to the other side. As soon as he was back on his feet, Randall grabbed his arm and dragged him out of the room.

The figure twisted its head, watching them leave with those gaping, hollow eyes.

"What about Caroline?" Randall gasped.

Nathan shook his head, unable to tear his eyes away from the thing that was watching them. It made no move to go after them, just kept staring at them with that smile.

"We'll have to come back for her."

They found Lucy and Avery in the sitting room by the unlit fire. Their faces were cast in shades of grey, and Avery was breathing heavily between her legs, her skin slick with sweat.

"What the hell was that thing?" She gasped, pushing her hair back from her face as perspiration beaded her brow. "D-did you see it? Oh, god."

"Where's Caroline?" Lucy asked when the others came in.

"She's still back there. She's in some kind of… weird trance. I didn't know what to do."

Lucy gritted her teeth, standing up suddenly. "We need to go and get her. We can't leave her there." She marched past them both with a determined frown, but Nathan quickly caught her arm.

"Wait, let's go together."

Randall helped Avery back to her feet, and the four of them returned to the study, peering cautiously inside.

The room was now warm and bright with the sunlight peeking through the windows. Caroline had opened up the drapes and blown out all of the candles, and was now humming quietly to herself as she packed away her equipment. She didn't seem to notice them watching her until they called for her attention.

"Caroline?" Lucy said tentatively, the others shuffling around her in confusion.

"Hey guys!" Caroline said, grinning at them. Her voice was unusually cheerful, and there was colour in her cheeks for the first time since they'd gotten there. "Wasn't that fun?"

The four podcasters exchanged another wary glance. "Uh, Caroline? How are you… feeling?" Randall asked uncertainly.

"I'm feeling fine! Much better, thank you," she said, her grin widening to show more of her teeth.

Avery nudged Randall. "I don't like this," she whispered, keeping her voice low. "Something doesn't feel right."

Randall shook his head, not taking his eyes off the psychic. "I agree."

Caroline paused and patted her stomach. "You know what, I'm famished! How about we get some dinner on the go?"

Avery didn't have much of an appetite that evening, but she forced herself to eat simply for the strength it would give her. The last three days had been more exhausting than she'd ever experienced before, and for the first time since she'd started doing paranormal investigations, she couldn't wait to get out of there.

The others seemed equally fatigued. When she looked across the table, all she saw were wan faces and heavy eyes. Lucy and the others hadn't touched much of their food either, pushing it absently around their plate.

Caroline, however, seemed to be in good spirits. Her sudden recovery after earlier tugged a little at Avery's subconscious, but she forced herself not to think too much on it. If something was wrong, the psychic would tell them.

“I think it’ll be another early night for us,” Lucy said, breaking the silence around the table. She smiled thinly. “I feel so drained after today.”

Randall nodded. “Me too. Maybe we could finish reviewing our footage in the morning and hold the final podcast session then. John isn’t coming for us until the afternoon anyway. We’ll have plenty of time to pack away our things and get ready to leave. I really don’t think I can stay awake much longer.”

“Sounds good to me,” Nathan said, stretching his arms out behind him with a yawn and blinking away the veneer of fatigue clouding his eyes. “We’ve got some good evidence, but I’m looking forward to getting out of here. It’s been a pretty rough investigation this time around.”

There was a unanimous murmur of agreement around the table.

Caroline said nothing, staring ruminatively down at her hands, cradled in her lap.

“Well, I’m heading up to bed,” Lucy said, pushing back her chair. “Hope you all sleep well. See you in the morning.”

She walked off yawning, and the others listened to her footsteps recede up the stairs. A moment later, a door clicked shut.

"You sure you're feeling alright, Caroline?" Randall asked, flicking a glance towards the psychic.

She seemed to spring back to life, nodding enthusiastically. "Perfectly fine." She clinked her cutlery against the side of the plate, reaching up to dab the corner of her lips with her fingers. She was the only one who'd had the appetite to finish her meal.

Randall narrowed his eyes slightly at her fervent behaviour, but didn't push her with any further questions. Like Avery, he probably didn't want to dash the good mood that had suddenly sprung upon her.

"Alright, well, goodnight to you all," he said eventually, standing up from his chair. Nathan and Avery followed suit, but Caroline stayed where she was. "You not coming?"

"I'm going to finish cleaning up down here," she said, stacking their plates together absently. "I won't be too much longer."

Her cheeks sunk into another careless grin, and the others shrugged as they left, disappearing through the door.

Now alone in the sitting room, with the fire almost burnt out, Caroline dropped the plates she was holding and turned back to the corner, where the shadows seemed to gather with unusual thickness.

For a moment, she thought she saw a face peering back.

That night, Caroline was woken up by the same thudding noise as before. She sat up, clutching the blankets tightly between her fists, and listened to what sounded like someone running up and down the staircase.

Whoever it was, it seemed to want their attention.

When she heard nobody else's door open, she got out of bed, pulling on a jacket as the chilly air touched her arms.

Forgoing socks or shoes, she padded on tiptoes over to the door, chasing away shadows with a half-lidded gaze. The night felt darker than usual. She could barely see her arms as she stretched them out in front of her, reaching for the handle.

Touching the cool metal in the dark, she pulled it open and stepped out.

The thudding noises stopped abruptly, barely an echo lingering.

She wavered in the silence.

"Someone out there?" She called, squinting against the gloom. "Hello?"

She moved forward, the floorboards creaking faintly beneath her feet as she curled her toes against the cold floor.

As she walked down the hallway, the air seemed to change. It grew heavy and cold, forming a layer of discomfort on her skin.

She could barely see a thing. She felt forward with her hands, running her fingertips along the peeling walls to make sure she didn't bump into anything.

"Hello?" She said again, her voice receding into the dark. "Is there someone out here?"

As she approached the top of the staircase, she became aware of something in the dark with her. She wasn't alone.

"Is there someone here who wants to speak with me?" She asked, lowering her voice again. She stood at the top of the stairs, looking down into the pooling shadows. "I'm listening, if you have something to say."

She waited for several minutes, standing in the cold air and listening for anything amongst the silence that might tell her what the spirit wanted.

"I'd like to help you," she said. "If you'll let me."

Something fell against the back of her neck – a whisper, or a breath, stirring her hair against her skin.

The muscles in her shoulders clenched, and she turned slowly, holding her breath.

A man was standing behind her, close enough that she could smell the rot on his breath. He had no eyes, only empty sockets that bled like shadows, and his skin was thin enough that she could see the sharp angles of his bones.

She gasped softly as his shrunken lips parted, and something pushed through from the inside. The pale tip of a worm's head poked out from between his lips, writhing down his chin, and falling to the floor at Caroline's feet. A second later, more worms appeared, poking the air blindly as they pushed out through his lips and the empty sockets of his eyes.

A raspy voice said: "Catch… you."

Then the man's hands shot forward, connecting with Caroline's shoulders.

He shoved her back, and she lost her footing. All of a sudden, there was nothing beneath her but air. She felt weightless. Her stomach flipped.

Then the ground came rushing up to meet her.

The first impact shattered her ribs. Pain tore through her body. The next one broke her arm and she screamed as the man grinned at her from the top of the steps.

Then her head snapped against the banister of the staircase and she plunged into darkness.

The scream reached Lucy through her dreams, yanking her awake.

She gasped, blinking rapidly as the darkness swelled around her. She was covered in a sheen of sweat, her hair sticking uncomfortably against her skin. With a quiet groan, she tried to reach up to brush the hair out of her face… and realised she couldn't. Her arms wouldn't move. With panicked breaths, she tried moving the rest of her body, but it wouldn't listen either. She was paralysed.

She was lying slightly on her side, her arm trapped beneath the pillow, and when she raised her eyes to look for Avery, she saw the covers thrown back and the bed empty.

Where had she gone?

"A-Avery?" She whispered, her voice a low croak as she tried to turn her head to look around the room. "Avery?"

She received no response, and she felt panic seize her. She was alone.

She whimpered quietly, trying to conjure feeling in her limbs, but they wouldn't move. Everything felt numb.

Then something touched her. The clammy brush of a finger against her cheek. Her heart thudded harder in her chest, and she choked out another cry.

What was happening? Why couldn't she move?

The touch retreated, but she still felt as though there was something in the room with her. A nameless, faceless shadow. Something in the dark.

Fighting against the stiffness of her neck, she managed to turn her head slowly. Hair tumbled out of her eyes, and she lifted her gaze up at the ceiling.

A face stared back.

There was a figure on the ceiling, watching her with dark eyes and a smile far too large for its face. Something about it seemed disproportionate in the shadows, as though its arms and legs were too long, protruding unnaturally from its joints. When it opened its mouth, sharp, thorn-like teeth glinted in the dark, and Lucy screamed.

The scream was cut short to a low-throated moan as the entity above her reached out with long, gangly arms and wrapped them around her throat, choking her.

Her lungs burned and she willed herself to move, to push the entity's arms away, but she couldn't. Her whole body was frozen, and she could do nothing as the thing continued to strangle her, its fingers tightening around her neck.

That long, gruesome smile was the last thing she saw before darkness hooded over her eyes and her chest failed to rise.

Nathan blinked listlessly against the darkness of his room. A door slamming shut had dragged him out of his sleep, and now he waited for the haze to clear from his mind, his eyes flickering over the rafters of the ceiling.

The door… who had slammed the door?

That's what had woken him up, hadn't it? Was there someone moving around the house, at this time of night?

He sat up sluggishly, trying to shake away the fatigue still heavy in his bones. He'd been dreaming about something, but he couldn't remember what. Whatever it was had left a bad taste on his tongue, though, and a flutter of unease in his chest.

But now he was awake, and it was almost like his dreams had bled into reality, merging together so that he couldn't tell if his mind was awake or asleep.

So… who had slammed the door?

It had sounded close. Enough to rattle the doorframe of his own room and yank him out of his dreams.

His room was more apart than the others. The only place that was close by was the one directly opposite him – the old operating room. But why would someone go in there?

Driven by his own confusion, Nathan picked himself out of bed and stumbled towards the door, his body still trapped in the groggy state of sleep.

Slipping out through the door, he glanced left and right. He couldn't see anyone else out of bed. Nor could he hear any movement.

His eyes landed on the door opposite. Even in the dark, he could see the outline against the wall, the ridge of the handle, the metal glinting with an unnatural light.

Was there somebody in there?

Moving quietly on his tiptoes, he went towards the old operating room, twisting the handle with fingers damp with sweat. It opened noiselessly, shadows bleeding out along his feet that seemed darker than the rest.

Driven by some kind of compulsion, he stepped inside.

A cold, clammy wind immediately gusted through the room, slamming the door shut behind him, an echo of the noise he had heard earlier.

Nathan realised the balcony doors had been thrown wide open, clanging and scraping against their hinges as the breeze blew through.

On the other side, balancing on the railings outside with their back facing him, was Avery.

His eyes went wide. "Avery! What the hell are you doing?" He shouted, snapping out of his drowsiness and rushing forward. "Get down from there."

She turned slowly to face him, her toes curling around the railings as she cocked her head playfully to the side.

When he saw her face, he seized up.

Her eyes were pitch black, as hollow as the shadows around the room. Black veins ran below the surface of her skin, protruding from her neck and temples. When she opened her mouth, darkness flooded out.

"Goodbye Nathan," she said, her voice a low, demonic growl. Then she threw out her arms and fell backwards, her feet slipping off the balcony as she disappeared below.

Nathan screamed, running forward and catching himself against the railings. On the ground below, Avery's body lay twisted and mangled, blood spreading along the gravel in a dark puddle.

"Oh god," he whispered, covering his mouth as staggered back into the room. The gruesome image of Avery's body, twisted and bloody on the ground, hovered in his mind. "We have to get out of here."

Filled with horror, he turned round towards the door, and froze.

He wasn't alone.

The doctor from his dreams was stood behind him, blocking the doorway. In one hand, he held a long lobotomy needle, its tip red with blood, and in the other, a hammer. An unnaturally long grin stretched along his face.

"Catch you," he whispered.

Nathan screamed again, almost tripping over his own feet as he stumbled to get away.

Hands grabbed his shoulders from behind, and he realised there were more of them. Doctors with white coats and wide grins, surrounding him from every angle. He found himself being dragged onto the bed in the corner of the room, strapped down by those same shackles from his dream as the doctors leered over him.

One of them grabbed his hand, yanking it towards the pair of pliers he was holding, and he screamed as the first fingernail was torn from his skin.

Another one pressed a stethoscope to his chest, laughing hysterically. "*Badump, badump*," he said in a mocking tone. "Listen to how fast your heart is going! At this rate, you might have a heart attack." He burst into manic laughter again as Nathan writhed and screamed, trying to escape the bonds strapping him down.

The door to the room suddenly flew open, and Nathan saw Randall standing there, framed by shadows. His face turned a grisly shade of white when he glimpsed Nathan, strapped down on the bed.

"Randall!" He screamed, but his voice was drowned out beneath the doctors' laughter.

"Stay still," the doctor sneered, bringing the needle down to his eye. "This might hurt a little."

Then he drove the hammer home, and Nathan went still.

Randall sobbed hysterically as he ran from the room. In his mind, he saw Nathan's body jerk once and then fall still, the doctors laughing gleefully around him.

He was dead. Oh god, he was dead.

He had to get the others and get out of there.

Ramming his shoulder against the door to Lucy and Avery's room, he stumbled inside screaming for them to get up.

The words died on his lips when he saw Lucy. She was lying in bed, her neck twisted at an impossible angle, staring at him with wide, dead eyes.

"No no no no," he cried, tearing his hands through his hair when he saw Avery's bed was empty. "Why did this have to happen?"

Leaving behind the gruesome sight, he rushed down to Caroline's room, finding it empty too. Where had they both gone? Had they managed to escape?

Through vision blurred with tears and sweat, Randall stumbled down the stairs, his footsteps thundering against the wood.

When he reached the bottom, his shoes connected with something soft and he was thrown forward, landing hard on his hands and knees.

Gasping wildly, he twisted round and saw Caroline's blank face staring back. Her neck was broken, and her body was crumpled beneath her, blood trickling down from her mouth.

Dead.

They were all dead.

"Oh god," he cried, pushing himself to his feet with trembling hands. "Why is this happening? Why is this happening?!"

Each breath burned as it pushed through his lungs, and he could hear nothing above the thundering of his heart. He staggered into the sitting room, trying not to focus on the things watching him from the dark, and grabbed his laptop.

He booted up the webcam, hoping desperately that someone would see his stream and get some help to them, before it was too late for him.

But when he tried to record, nothing happened.

Instead, a video clip started playing.

It was him. He was sitting exactly where he was now, sweat pouring down his forehead, his breathing sharp and panicked. Only it was different. In the video, he was screaming for someone to help him, asking whoever was listening to call the police, anyone.

As Randall watched, the shadows in the video began to come alive. Faces appeared in the gloom around them, and the shadows formed bodies, reaching out long appendages as they slowly engulfed him and his screams into complete darkness.

The clip stopped, and in the live webcam screen, he saw his face exactly as it had been in the video, pale and terrified.

Something moved behind him.

He twisted round, and the shadows started to move.

Danica fixed her fringe and smoothed down her shirt before she hit record, plastering a smile onto her face. "Hey there, Darers, it's Danica from *Dare Danica*. Today, I'm asking you, my viewers, to choose the dare that I'll be doing this week. That's right, I'm leaving it entirely up to you. So drop a comment below and I'll pick one of your suggestions."

As she kept an eye on the chat, she saw that the comments were already flooding in.

I dare you to steal your neighbour's dog.

Drink a whole bottle of ketchup… lol.

Dare you to dye your hair bright green!

She scrolled through them, dismissing the ones she'd already done or ones that sounded silly, until one caught her eye.

I dare you to spend a night at Redburn Manor by yourself, with nothing but a camera to log that you actually completed the dare.

She read it out loud, her eyebrows arching thinly. "A night at Redburn Manor, huh?" She said, then burst into mocking laughter. "You think I believe in ghosts? Pfft, fine. I'll do it. I'm not scared of a few measly rumours."

Another commenter responded: *Anyone who goes there either commits suicide or is murdered. It's dangerous.*

Danica rolled her eyes. "Didn't you read the headlines? That's all hogwash. That podcasting group wasn't killed by ghosts. That crazy chick Avery murdered them all, then jumped off the balcony to kill herself. It's just some old, abandoned house."

She scrolled through the rest of the comments. Most of them believed she was right, but there were a few who seemed adamant the place really was haunted.

Danica grinned. She'd show them they were wrong.

"Alright then. Redburn Manor it is. On my own with only a camera. Sounds easy enough. It might even be fun, exploring an empty house at night."

She received mixed admiration and concern from her commenters, some of them warning her not to do anything too reckless, but she ignored them. What was the point of her blog if she wasn't going to do the dares people asked her to do?

"You guys worry too much," she scoffed, flicking her fringe out of her eyes. "I'll be fine. After all, what can go wrong in a house that's been abandoned for almost a decade?"

It used to be an asylum. People died there.

"Do you know how many people die in their own homes?" She said dismissively. "Stop trying to convince me not to go. Danica had chosen her dare, and she can't go back. Those are the rules! And I've never forfeited a dare, so I'm not about to start now."

After chatting with her commenters for another half an hour, she signed off and ended the video feed, feeling the usual thrum of nervous excitement from doing a dare. She had all week to complete the challenge, but part of her was still caught up in the initial excitement, and she'd already made the decision to go tonight. This was her chance to prove to her viewers that she wasn't afraid of a little haunted house. Stuff like this always went viral. Maybe *Dare Danica* would finally get the recognition she knew it deserved.

Reaching into her closet, she pulled out an overnight bag and began to pack, throwing in everything she figured she would need; her coat, a flashlight and her night vision camera.

Satisfied she had everything she needed, she threw open her bedroom door and shouted down to her mom: "Hey, mom! Is it okay if I spend the night at a friend's house tonight?"

"Which friend?" Her mom yelled back up the stairs.

"Alice," Danica blurted, hoping her mom didn't have any need to call Alice's mom in the meantime. She would be grounded for life if her mom knew she was sneaking out to spend the night alone at an abandoned house. She only had limited knowledge of her blog at all.

"Okay. But make sure you're back by ten in the morning. We're visiting your grandma for lunch."

"Sure, mom!"

Danica closed the door and grinned to herself.

Redburn Manor, you better get ready. Because here I come.

TH
HAUNTI
OF
EMILY BLAKE

SNEAK PEAK

(A Novel - Coming 2021)

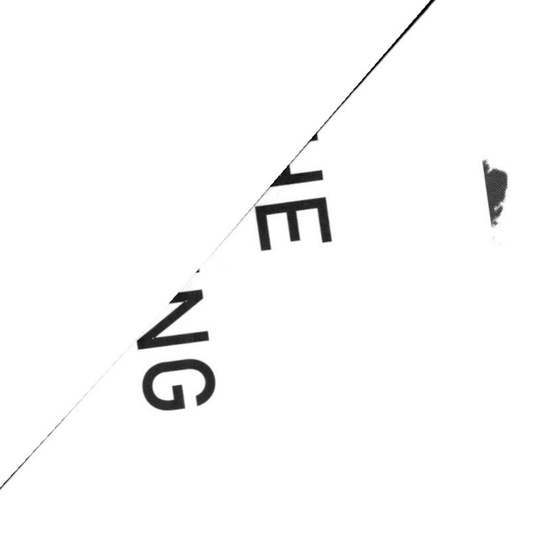

hrough a

... for it to

... it had taken them almost twenty minutes to find this road if you could call it that. Out here it was hard to tell the difference between a path and just a place where a tree wasn't growing. Finally, Emily had found a small cut through the thick trunks and had been crawling along what she hoped was the driveway for the past ten minutes. A little unsure of her decision, Emily nursed her bottom lip with light nibbles. If she had been mistaken it was going to be near impossible to turn around without hitting something.

Emily leaned forward nearly pressing herself against the steering wheel. "I think it's starting to thin out."

This being the third time she'd said the same exact words and only uncomfortable silence greeted her. Joy, who usually was the loquacious one, remained silent. This time however, the words proved to be accurate. They emerged from the trees into a meadow covered in wild grasses. They bent and swayed in the wind making it seem as if the ground itself was golden body of water.

"See, I told you it was clearing up." Emily said.

James leaned forward between the gap in the front seats. "You were bound to be right eventually, Em.”

Emily narrowed her eyes at him in mock anger. "With that attitude I should have left you behind."

"You wouldn't have left me. Besides, you two would be bored by yourselves with only each other to talk to."

Joy looked up from her laptop. "So, I've been trying to find some information on this place... what?"

James fell back into his seat in the rear of the car laughing. "See what I mean? My sis, always the life of the party."

Joy spun back to face him. "What? You mean I'm boring? Just because I want to know..."

"Dear lord." At the sound of Emily's voice, they both crossed their arms and veered out their separate windows.

They stopped on the crest of a small rise giving them a panoramic view of house and the grounds surrounding it. It stood two stories tall with two windows jutting out of the front of its second story. Even in the midday light the windows were dim making the structure look pale in comparison.

Vines and weeds had fled their boundaries and intermixed with grass that had intruded from the field overtaking what had once been the front of the home. Most of the vegetation appeared to be in the throes of death, starved of life-giving nutrients upon a spoiled tract of land.

The paint that at one time had coated the outside had flaked away, scored from the walls by wind driven dust and rain. The corrugated roof was more rust than anything that resembled metal leaving questions as to what protection it offered. If this place had been welcoming to visitors those days were in the past. Now it served as a stark reminder of the irrevocable pursuit of nature to reclaim and return the land to what once was.

"We're staying there?" James tapped lightly on the glass. This was far from the country getaway that he had expected when Emily and his sister offered to let him come with them. "Where did you two find this place?"

Lost in the moment Emily appeared not to hear what he had said. "It's perfect."

James however heard her perfectly and stuck his head between the seats once more. "Um, what? This place is a complete dump, it doesn't even seem like it has power. Joy, how do you plan on using your laptop?"

"The place has a generator out back, at least that's what the information I could find out about it before we rented it said." Joy told him.

James looked back and forth between them and collapsed back into his seat. "You two have lost it. Completely mental."

The road leading to the house became increasingly rough and the truck bounced and vibrated as the tires rolled over the washboards and pits that littered the surface. They rounded one final corner and pulled to a stop. The building seemed to loom above them in silent challenge. The deterioration on the outside was even more apparent from this distance as even the smaller blemishes became visible. Up close the house drew them in, it was as if the harder they tried to gaze away the more they had to stare it.

"Well, how about we go check out the inside?" Emily asked them both as she pulled the keys from the ignition.

James craned his neck to see the building out the front of the truck windshield. "Or we could go back and find a hotel to stay in."

Joy rolled her eyes and shut her laptop. "Oh, I'm sure glad we brought along a big strong man to keep us womenfolk safe." she said in her best southern accent.

Emily laughed at the offended look James gave his sister. "Come on James, where's your sense of adventure?"

With that Emily opened her door and got out of the SUV. She stretched trying to ease the stiffness of driving from her limbs. "I mean look at this place. It's freaking awesome!"

James looked down the length of the building unconvinced of really what to think. "What kind of person would want to live in a place like this?"

Joy walked by her brother and patted him gently on the back. "Obviously, someone rugged and tough, something that you know nothing about."

"Hey what's that supposed to mean?"

Joy glanced over her shoulder at her older sibling with her lip stuck out in an exaggerated pout. "Oh, did I offend your delicate sensibilities?"

"Are you going to just stand there or are we going to check this place out?" Emily began picking her way through the dense ground cover towards the front door. Halfway there she spun around and beckoned them to join her. "Come on you two."

Joy captured the front of her brother's shirt and dragged him forward, he didn’t fight her, but a look of reservation clouded his face.

Emily and Joy climbed the two wood steps leading to the small landing where the front door stood. Joy reached into her pocket and produced a key. Surprisingly, it is modern rather than something that would more suit a home of its age.

Sliding the key into the cylinder Emily paused and looked back at her two friends. "Are we ready?"

The key turned smoothly in the lock and the door swung open silently on its hinges revealing the first few feet of a darkened room. Emily was the first to pass the threshold into the house followed by Joy. The room was dim, but the windows let in enough light to for them to see the general layout. Dust floated about the place on unseen currents, the tiny bits of the past that had lain dormant upon every surface and in every corner until life was present once more.

Emily thought of it as the house finally drawing in a long-awaited breath now that the door was finally open.

A set of wooden plank stairs rose in the center of the room leading to the upper floor of the building. To their right was a primitive kitchen complete with a woodfire stove against one wall. A few cupboards had been hung above the counter for storage. Near one of the windows where a family could look out while enjoying their meal a small round table stood with four chairs.

To the left was a room that probably once was a living room. A few chairs had been arranged haphazardly around the room. They were all straight-back and made of wood, more for utility than comfort. A large worn rug, the original color long since faded covered the center of the floor. On the wall hung a large cross about two feet tall and half as much wide between two oval frames that contained yellowing portraits of an elderly man and woman that appeared to be staring at each other.

James stepped into the room next to Emily and took in the scene. "I'm going to have to find out who their decorator is."

Emily elbowed him in the ribs for the sarcastic remark. "Just go start bringing in our stuff."

He shook his head and strode back out the door leaving Emily and Joy standing just inside the doorway by themselves.

"So how about you check out the rooms upstairs and I see what else is down here?" Joy asked Emily.

"That works, when you see James can you have him drop my stuff upstairs so I can get set up?" Emily responded still admiring the interior.

"Yup, when I see him, I'll send him up." Joy waved and took off down the hallway.

With every step up the stairs the wood had let out an audible creaking noise. Emily ran her hand along the railing feeling the surface of the wood that had been worn smooth from age. As she climbed higher, the walls closed in around her the amplifying the noise making it appear louder than before.

After a few more steps up, a hallway came into view. It was darker up here and she could only see a solitary door on either side of the passage. The upper floor was silent, Emily couldn't even hear Joy moving around the level below her. Behind her one of the stairs let out a creak as if someone had put their weight on it. She turned around to glance down the stairs only to see them vacant. *Just the house settling. It's old and we're bound to hear a noise or two during the time we're here.*

The air up here was heavier and carried with it the scent of aged wood almost like she was standing in the loft of an ancient barn. There hadn't been a lot of open floor on the landing making the space feel cramped even with just her standing there. So far everything about this house seemed to be designed for a person to be uncomfortable.

With only ambient light to see by, Emily strained to see through the dense shadows that enveloped the rest of the hall. With this in mind she decided to begin with the door closest to her. She moved up to the door on the right side of the hall and tried its handle. Like the front door, it moved without resistance and the door slid open.

Emily tentatively eased into the dark space edging towards the dim outline of light that seeped around the edges of the window. She probed the area in front of her with a hand swinging it back and forth as she cautiously moved further into the bedroom. As she reached the window Emily took hold of the curtains and drew them open. The windows were coated with dust, but enough light was let in to reveal the contents of the room. The room was small and except for an old wooden bedframe that appeared to be only large enough for a child the room is empty. Her gaze scanned the room and she noticed even the walls bared no adornments. There wasn't even a dresser or a closet to store clothes. *It is more like a wooden cell than a bedroom,* Emily thought to herself with a slight shudder.

Leaving, Emily left the shades drawn and the door open to bring allow her to see better. Across the hall she found a similar room lacking any personal touches and even the most basic of furniture.

From down the hall she heard the sound of the stairs squeaking and something smacking into one of the walls followed by a loud thud on the floor of the landing. Curious as to what it was, she glanced around the door frame hesitantly only to see two suitcases on the ground and the back of James' head descending the stairs.

Emily cupped her hand to her mouth to call after him. "Thank you!"

She watched him raise his hand in acknowledgement before bobbing out of view. *Well, now I've just got to find a place to put them.*

Undeterred by the two rooms Emily began going door to door looking for a suitable place to call her own for the foreseeable future. With every failure her optimism waned a little further. She'd already checked eight rooms and none of them had anything but the bedframe in them. With only four more rooms to go it appeared like she would have to just make the best of one of the spartan rooms she'd already seen.

She opened the next door expecting to see much of the same. The room itself contained the same small bedframe as every other room but her attention was immediately deterred by something else, an aged desk sitting against the next to the window. This was what she had been looking for, truly it was the whole reason she'd come here in the first place. She'd needed a place to write and this home was to be her inspiration, a way to break through the dam that had been constructed in her mind, a way to silence the doubters.

When Emily first understood that she wanted to be a writer the seed of an idea was something that she barely had to nurture. Even the smallest ideas would take on a life of their own and flourish. It had been like a bottomless well that she could dip into any time she wanted. There had been so many ideas it would have been impossible for her to write them all.

This led to her publishing her first book *Without Sleep*. Only months after that her follow up book *If You Tell* hit shelves and within months became a *New York Times* Best Seller. She was considered one of the up-and-coming horror writers. Critics and fans alike praised her works and were anxious to see what she would come up with next.

For the past three years her mind had been a breeding ground for cobwebs and dead-end ideas. It wasn't as if the well had gone dry, it was worse than that. Emily seemed to have lost the well entirely. That part of her mind seemed shut off to her now and the pressure of a new release were mounting.

Sure, the Insta-followers with their constant questions of *"When's the next one coming out?"* or *"Are you going to write another one?"* seemed to build in quantity and frequency on a daily basis. Emily had found it somewhat simple to ignore the mounting questions as well as the weekly calls from her publisher as well. Those had all become easy to ignore. However, the comments that referred to her as a "passing fancy" or a "two-hit wonder" those she took personally. These criticisms shook her to her core, scolding her talent like smoldering blades. Emily wanted to prove to herself that she hadn't just gotten lucky with her first two books, that she could actually do this as a career.

She'd tried everything she could think of, even going to a shrink but nothing seemed to help. Emily was about to give up when her friend Joy had suggested that she try getting away, somewhere that she could just focus on the written word. Emily hadn't been completely convinced this would work, after all Joy, a fellow author and best friend, wrote about historic locations. Joy could go pretty much anywhere and find a story, whereas Emily relied on her imagination.

Without any better ideas though, Emily had agreed and had jumped in with both feet. Sure, this place was abandoned, run down, and more than a little creepy but that is the exact type of place that Emily wrote about. She needed this opportunity for inspiration almost as much as she needed air to breathe. It was an opportunity to immerse herself in a building right out of the pages of the story she wanted to write. So, she was determined to make the best of the prospect because if not she didn't know what she would do after this. Writing had always been Plan A, B and C. Not writing would be like losing her hands, she'd be incomplete.

Almost like she was in a trance Emily walked across the floor to the desk. It was a dark red, if the light hadn't been on it the color would have looked black. The surface although smooth was not a perfect rectangle. The front and back edges waved like someone had left the natural shape of the tree.

The legs were simple and without ornamentation, but they didn't detract from the overall beauty of the desk. It was an extraordinary example of craftsmanship.

Emily sat down in the chair and rubbed the top surface. The surface was impossibly smooth almost as if it were made of glass rather than wood. There was history here. She could feel it, memories had been infused into the very materials that surrounded her. What dreams did the people have when they stared through this very window out into the world beyond it? Emily closed her eyes and tried to see back into to the past.

An idea stirred in the back of her mind; it was barely a whisper, but it was there. It took her so much by surprise she let out a little gasp. It felt like seeing an old friend after a long absence. *I need my paper and pen. I have to get started before it's gone.*

Emily got up and half-jogged down the hallway to where James had left her suitcases. Grabbing the handles, she rolled them back to the bedroom bouncing along the floor in her haste. The larger of the two bags held her clothes, it was the smaller one of the two that she cared about at this very moment. She heaved it up on the bedframe and fumbled at the zipper, adrenaline making her hands clumsy.

Finally, she was able to grab hold of the tab and jerked it sideways. The zipper snagged on a piece of fabric as it tried to turn the corner bringing it to an abrupt halt. Emily yanked the piece of metal attempting to force it past the obstruction, but it seemed to only make it worse.

"Come on you piece of junk!" she yelled losing her patience, slapping at the bag in nearly resigned frustration.

Closing her eyes, she took a deep breath in through her nose and out through her mouth trying to calm herself. A little steadier now she backed the zipper up allowing it to move freely once more. Slowly this time she undid the top flap on the suitcase revealing several journals in which she wrote all of her stories and a worn silver pen, the same pen she had written her first two novels with. It was her good luck charm, even if it had failed her recently.

To her surprise the slight hiccup with opening the suitcase hadn't allowed the idea to dissipate in her mind. In fact, it has grown more solid, expanded even in plot and characters. Emily lifted out one of the identical books from the stack but held her hand in place in a moment of hesitation before taking her pen. Fear and doubt bubbled up from her belly and burnt into her chest. She softly shuddered as if shedding the layer of self-doubt, *I can do this. I know it.*

Emily drew the pen from the sleeve that held it in place feeling the familiar weight of it. She knew it was time to find out if she was a writer or an author. To her a writer simply put ink on paper, an author had an intimate relationship with the words she used. The pen wasn't the tool authors used to create with, the words were the instrument. When used correctly they could paint pictures no human eye had ever seen before. They created worlds that people would beg and plead to get lost in.

Emily sat at the desk pen in hand ready to begin. Against the dark wood of the desk the paper looked impossibly white, almost as if it were glowing. The prospect of filling a single page seemed daunting yet alone hundreds of them.

As soon as the pen touched the paper Emily was startled by James' voice. "Hey Emily!" She scrawled a jagged line down the center of the first page before the pen clatters to the floor between her feet. "Just wanted you to know that all our stuff is inside. Joy and I are going to get our rooms set up."

When Emily turned and seared a look at him, James held up both hands in defense and took a couple steps back. "Uh, sorry about that. I just wanted to..."

Emily stood and walked to him a tight smile upon her face. Reaching up she placed her finger on his forehead pushing him out the door. "Out." The word came out like a breath.

Closing the door, she returned to the desk and looked at the zigzagging line across the first page. She scowled in annoyance, *not a good way to start a book.*

Emily bent down to find her pen that had dropped when James had snuck up on her. She ran her eyes across the surface of the floor searching for the misplaced writing instrument but could not find it anywhere. "Where did you go?" As if talking to the inanimate object would make it somehow appear.

Emily crawled under the desk thinking she must have kicked it when she stood up. Emily froze in place as a metallic clink came from right above her head. Cautiously, she scootched back and rose up on her knees so she could see atop the desk. Sitting next to the open journal sat her missing pen.

Please remember to leave a review after reading.

Follow Eve S. Evans on instagram:
@eves.evansauthor

or

@foreverhauntedpodcast

Check out our Bone-Chilling Tales to keep you awake segment on youtube for more creepy, narriated and animated haunted stories by Eve S Evans.

Let me know on Instagram that you wrote a review and I'll send you a free copy of one of my other books!

Check out Eve on a weekly basis on one of her many podcasting ventures. Forever Haunted, The Ghosts That Haunt Me with Eve Evans, Bone Chilling Tales To Keep You Awake or A Truly Haunted Podcast. (On all podcasting networks.)

If you love to review books and would like a chance to snatch up one of Eve's ARCs before publication, follow her facebook page:

Eve S. Evans Author

For exclusive deals, ARCs, and giveaways!

From the time I was first published to current, (2021) I've learned so much about life and my journey into the paranormal.

I started this journey a few years ago after living in multiple haunted houses. However, it was one house in particular that chewed me up and spit me out you could say.

After residing in that house I wanted answers… needed them. So I began my journey of interviewing multiple people who too have been haunted. Any occuptaion, you name it, I've interviewed them.

What did I learn from my journey so far? I'm honestly not sure if I will ever get the answers I truly desire in this lifetime. However, I am determined not to stop anytime soon. I will keep plugging along, interviewing and ghost hunting. I am determined to find as many answers as I can in this lifetime before it too is my turn to be nothing but a ghost.

I have several books coming out this year and I am very well known for my "real ghost story anthologies", however, these will be mostly fictional haunted house books as I wanted to give myself a new challenge.

If you'd like to read one of my anthologies my reccomedation to start would be: True Ghost Stories of First Responders. In this book I interview police, firemen, 911 dispatchers and more. They share with me some of their creepiest calls that could possibly even be deemed "ghostly."

Also this year I am hoping to get my paranormal memoir out. I want to share my story and journey with everyone. Until then, just know that if you are terrified in your home or thinking you are going crazy with unexplained occurances, you ARE NOT alone. I thought I was going crazy too. But I wasn't.

If you'd like someone to talk to about what is going on in your home but don't know who to turn to, feel free to message me on Instagram or on Facebook.

Printed in Great Britain
by Amazon

83137304R00107